The Mental Pause

Memoirs of a Gorbal's Girl
By
Rusty Bernard

*This outpouring is dedicated to everyone who **still** loves me…………….
…..just the way I am!*

Mx

"Hello!"

Imagine if it was your job to listen to head cases like me all day. I've been with me all day, every day, for fifty-two years and it is exhausting. Some days I want to get away and there is nowhere to turn. Everywhere I go, there I am. If you happen to have me thrust upon you, with no way out, then I can assure you it's highly likely you might try to kill yourself.

Tam was my psychiatrist and there were times, after one of my visits, that I was seriously worried about his mental health and the effect I was having on him. The first time I met him he seemed quite stable.

"Good morning, my name is Tam Mullaney and I'm here to evaluate you this morning. I'll ask you some questions and if you could try to answer, as honestly as possible, that would be grand. If at any point you want to stop, just interrupt me and let me know. How does that sound?"

How fabulous, as soon as he starts talking bullshit I'll pull the plug on what seemed like a complete waste of time and energy; bit like myself actually. He seems quite pleasant with a hint of an Irish accent and a ready smile. He's wearing cord trousers and a nice check shirt with the top button open, showing a cluster of ginger, chest hair. The trainers are a tell-tale sign. He's not a real doctor you see because that's not what I need but he'll need them to high tail it out of here when I'm finished with him. Bet he's thinking;

"Here we go again, she'll either, one; pretend to be OK and try to weigh up what the best answer will be so she doesn't get sectioned, but still hold on to her benefits. Or two; conjure up insanity but just

save herself from incarceration in order to get bloody disability and it's my fucking job to decide if she is worth her weight in my tax contributions. OK, let's get started."

In a way I agreed with Tam about the tax money because I get so fed up with people saying how great our NHS is and it pisses me off when they say it's free. Why then is £246 coming out of my salary every month. It's not free for me. I've got a feeling Tam and I are going to get on fine; as long as I'm enjoying myself. You see, pretending to go along with this insanity is part of my plan to keep everyone quiet. There's nothing wrong with me. Not really. Well nothing that Tam and his clipboard can fix anyway.

"Sex?"

At least he's not asking any trick questions. That's what they do you know, they ask something simple and expect you to rant on about, well, I don't know but I'm going to stay focused and stick to the topic.

"Are you asking how do I feel about sex? Not sure I understand what you mean, sex in the biological sense? Well, I think sex is marvellous and has its advantages. If you think about it, none of us would exist if we didn't have sex, eh Tam, you or me; or anyone else for that matter?

Isn't it remarkable people have been doing it for so long and they're still so interested in it? Every single person I know has, at some time or another, been affected by it in some way, good or bad. I know people that have been married for ages and still enjoy it. Even Catholics! It's the education system you see. They're all stupid. I mean create, procreate, spawn and that's only the language. Did none of them ever go to a biology class?

Do you know what I can't understand Tam? People, women, who find themselves pregnant and it comes as a big surprise. For goodness sake. Have they never looked in a bloody dictionary? Even the people who see it as recreational should be aware of the literal consequences of a mishap. It is after all 'an essential element of human biology and psychology'. I read that in Wikipedia so it must be true. Tam, why do you think we indulge in something so important, with such life changing implications, without doing at least a bit of research?

No, becomes about emotion, uncontrollable passion and sometimes even love.

People start having sex and suddenly it's all drama and consequences. Everything starts to become complicated and messy but, know what Tam? When you're not taking part it it's pure theatre to watch, I'm not kidding. The way in which it transforms people and relationships is amazing to observe.

I don't mean that I actually like **watching** people 'do it' Tam, I'm speaking hypothetically. It's the way people are affected by 'it' that makes it interesting. I'm not saying I've never seen anyone doing it, I've indulged in my fair share of porn and in my view you're lucky if it lasts longer than a medium bowl of popcorn. It makes me really thirsty and I usually have to have a drink midway through. One time this bloody jobs worth didn't let me back in as I'd left my ticket on the seat. Do you like it Tam, popcorn I mean?

It's so tragic watching grown, confident, successful people being turned into grovelling, quivering, suicidal wrecks in the space of a couple of sexually charged encounters; astonishing to witness. If intercourse is supposed to be a method of communication, then why is it that so many people fall out after an intense sexual relationship? They could be friends for years and then, bang, they make the mistake of shagging and all they have left is awkwardness; a lost friendship and a possible visit to the STD clinic.

I had crabs once Tam, he said I'd caught it from the toilet. Don't remember having sexual relations with the toilet. In fact, I'm a hoverer, unless it's my toilet I never sit down. My 'fat china' has never touched a strange urinal. I have fallen over and clacked my head but I'm proud to say my butt never made contact with porcelain. Although, there was this time when this guy's crown came loose and stuck...

Are you OK Tam? You look a bit flushed.

Even in the old days it was the same, all sorrow and suffering. Take Keats for instance and that 'Ode to Melancholy'. The way he droned on, like a girl, spewing out his anguish was sickening. I think that it was, in fact, about frustration and erectile dysfunction.

All that talk about, 'droop-headed flowers' was probably reflective of his performance and that's why he wrote about how much he depended on a 'strenuous tongue' to save the day. I do think he was a romantic and a dreamer who hoped for a 'wealth of globed peonies', which was probably a euphemism for hopeful vaginas. Then he went on and on about the juice of a burst grape and he wasn't talking about wine. God's sake they skirted around the issue of sex constantly without ever actually mentioning SEX!

Well, Tam, what would you have said to him Tam? "Stop bloody writing ya daft bugger and go see to your Fanny!" She must have been a saint to put up with all that shit.

Literary intellectuals can say what they like about it but maybe, just maybe, if his Fanny had written her response then it would have been entitled 'Owed an Orgasm'.

Sometimes I think sex is a bit like garlic. Some folk say it's medicinal but it's the smell that's harder to describe. The garlic I mean Tam. You can tell straight away if someone has been eating garlic because the scent is so distinctive but when someone has just had sex you can't be quite as sure. I could sense the whiff of a shag but could never put it into words.

It's almost like the smell on your hands after taking off rubber gloves, or a lint dressing. I once emptied my wardrobe and tied 10 bags of rubbish in black bin bags and the smell lingered on my hands for hours. I kept sniffing it while watching telly, I couldn't help myself. It was sort of comforting; the smell of reminded me of my husband when he came in from work. I never asked what he had been doing, although I knew, I always knew!

Tam do you know garlic isn't the only cooking ingredient that can be used as medicine. Rosemary is really good at nipping a headache in the bud and is nearly as effective as sex for getting rid of a sore head. Given the choice, I would rather have rosemary and garlic dressing with roast chicken than sex. The thing is if you don't have an orgasm you're left feeling like a tense, taut maniac who wants to kill the guilty inseminator. Men are selfish bastards aren't they Tam?

Do you know what else I think Tam? Sex is a very valuable incentive to get things done and in that case there's not much requirement for sexual gratification on the part of the recipient. My trick is to basically, take a deep breath and think of a new bathroom or a bookshelf that needs to be levelled. Used as currency sex can save a fortune on household maintenance and DIY. What do you prefer Tam sex or DIY? It's a win win situation if you like both and swing both ways! Imagine two gay guys who love sex and DIY! They would be as happy as pigs in shit. Sorry Tam I don't mean for a moment that homosexuals are pigs so don't think I was trying to, well, I mean, you've got those cords on so you're obviously not, you know?

Anyway, back to, yes, sex, I've used it to repair someone's ego. Sometimes, if I've made a cruel remark, or taken an argument or insult too far, I can usually wipe out all traces with a quick sexual exchange. Sometimes, you just have to pay up in order get things done and receive a bonus for yourself at the same time.

Tam, you look a bit baffled. Are you shocked by how calculating my thoughts on the subject are? Oh my goodness, I've just realised that I've been prostituting myself for next to nothing for the thirty odd years.

Hope you learn from this Tam and use what I'm telling you in order to, maybe, take advantage of a situation in the future. What you need to take into account is when it comes to sex, if you are the giver, then it is much easier as there's seldom very much emotion attached. It's usually the receiver who suffers the consequences i.e. crabs, pregnancy, chlamydia etc. etc. etc.!

Are you okay; you look as if your eyes are about to pop out?

Oh I'm sorry Tam, I just assumed that you were always on the giving end of things but if you are also on the receiving end then that makes things a bit more complicated and I don't really have much advice to give you on that score. Maybe you should ask one of your colleagues...

Anyway, in my very limited experience, when too much emotion is involved then sex can be very destructive and I try to remain sentimentally detached from it. It *was* "sex" you were asking about wasn't it? Or did you mean gender? Is it not pretty obvious that I am, in fact, a woman and I do in fact have a woman's name.

Although these days it's sometimes hard to tell isn't it? Do you think my hair is too short Tam, is that what it is?

A plain Glasgow girl.
An old Glasgow pub.
Come along and enjoy.
A drink and some grub.

That's what I wrote Tam, on my invitations, for my 40th birthday. I'm a shoe size five, dress size ten, medium height and build. Get the picture Tam? Plain, average maybe they should've called me Jane.

It's not that I suffer from low self-esteem or anything but where I come from, to be different, was to be isolated and bullied, so I've always tried to blend in and not draw attention to myself because oh, my, lord, Tam, the bright ginger hair was enough to contend with.

I did get myself into some pickles when I was young though; with my daydreaming and vivid imagination. I remember on the first day of school deciding, much to everyone's amusement, to call the priest Daddy instead of Father. That little gem got everyone's attention!

All four of us had, what my mum described as, the most magnificent heads of shining, golden hair and she constantly told us we had been blessed by angels. I was the only one who actually believed her though but what I didn't believe was that I'd been born into that family. I thought there'd been some mistake at the hospital and someday, soon, my real family would come and get me and take me off, into the sunset but until that day came I was prepared to make the most of it and let the angels watch over me.

We were almost like freaks of nature; Irish Catholic living in a

Scottish enclave of an Orange Institution. Nuneaton Street in Bridgeton was a hotbed of Protestantism but we were in hiding, from my dad and we knew that he would be guarded about entering hostile territory. We stayed with a friend of my mum's and so we wouldn't raise suspicion my sister and I decided to call our brothers Billie and Willie. How smart was that? You really have to have your wits about you when you are part of a puppet organisation being sponsored by the opposition.

It was like the march of the Red Brigade when we were out together. There was safety in numbers so we never left the house alone. All four of us, two brothers and two sisters, were a force to be damned with. Even though my mother told us how special we were, there was no denying that we had a fight on our hands. I often wondered where those blessed, bloody angels where when needed them. Every fucking day we were faced with King Billy's East End division. The Gaza strip had nothing on the orange line we had to cross every morning going to school.

On rainy days do you know what I would do Tam? I would sit and trace the raindrops on the window and pretend my tears belonged to someone else. I would look out, into the world and wondering what was out there for me. I dreamt of another life where I could dance and read and not be told off for trying to be smart. I longed to laugh 'til my belly ached and not be anxious about the tears that would inevitably follow. Like Oliver Twist I waited to be collected by my real kin but in the meantime I escaped into stories and drifted off onto my very own cloud.

My imagination was always a means of escape and I would drift away into a world where I didn't have to share my knickers or go to school with wet socks because the only pair I had were still sodden from the night before.

It would have been wonderful to have a dress with a receipt stating; previous owners. Honestly I would have worn it on the outside of the dress to let people know it was new. To clean my teeth with a brush and not my finger and carbolic soap would have been delightful. I don't think I used toothpaste until I was about eight. They, the sisters, said the soap was to stop us from swearing and the priest would take care of absolving actual and venial sins. The soapy lather was meant to take care of oral mischief and no one actually cared about the state of our choppers.

When I was six one of my dreams nearly came true when my mum asked a lady she knew to make dresses for us because she wanted to get a family picture taken. I was so excited that I couldn't stop talking about it and could hardly sleep and when I did I dreamt of puffed sleeves and full, swishy skirts. When the day came to get the photo taken we were all up really early. My mum took the candlewick bedspread and placed it over the worn couch in preparation for the photographer's 'shoot'.

The resulting portrait was the most horrendous thing imaginable and so was the dress and I dearly wished that someone had taken an actual shot at me with a gun instead of a camera. We lived just around the corner from Templeton's carpet factory and I'm sure they got the material for the dresses from an old skip round there. After two hours in it I was in absolute agony and covered in weals. It was like a scene from Medea, you know the one where she dies at the altar, foaming at the mouth because of the poison in the dress. I swear to God it was the most horrific experience and I never asked for anything 'new' again. It would have been less painful to be embalmed with formaldehyde and buried alive than to have had that picture taken.

The photo was horrific. My sister had lost her specs the day before and one of her eyes was turned to the back of her head and the boys, who were wearing matching shorts by the way, looked as if someone had asked them to chew a mouse and then ordered them to smile. I had been scratching myself so much because of the dress that I looked purple and my eyes were all puffy from lack of sleep because of the lack of sleep and excitement in anticipation of the dress.

Do you know what eventually saved me Tam? The library. One of the first books I read there was *'Anne of Green Gables'* and I remember feeling so happy for Anne when Marilla was taking her back to the orphanage. I was like the antithesis of Anne in that I longed for the order and security an institution would give. I used to make lists in my head of the luxuries I would have: a bed of my own, a toothbrush, breakfast, lunch and dinner. Oh, and nice, soft toilet paper because we only ever had newspaper or that scratchy San Izal stuff. Nothing worse than an itchy arsehole eh Tam?

Oh, by the way, I wasn't the only one who called that priest Daddy. Sometimes that's how he referred to himself. My brother's pal told us a story about when he was an altar boy and how, after mass on a Sunday, Father Anonymous used to give him sixpence to sit on his knee when they were alone in the vestry.

"Come and sit on Daddy's knee." he would say and tell him how special he was but warned him that if he told anyone else then Jesus would punish him. I don't have ownership of that whopper of a tale

so I'll stick to my secrets…and I promise to tell you almost everything!

"How are you feeling now?"

I'm not great today Tam but then, I suppose, that's to be expected. I've been locked in despair and gloom for so long the prospect of hope has me drowning in possibilities and it's scaring the shit out of me. Everyone is so fucking happy at the likelihood I'll 'get better' and it's driving me nuts but that's not the point is it Tam? I feel as if I'm careering the wrong way down a one-way street when everyone else is on a dual carriageway. They are all waving and smiling, listening to smooth fucking radio while I'm heading for a wall listening to 'Shut Up' by Madness on my iPod with the volume at 150 decibels.

I used to be like Wonder Woman Tam and now hardly have the power to get dressed. I don't think I really meant to kill myself, but then, here I am, with you and your clipboard and your questions. It's so sad. Not the clipboard thing but what I've done to my family. It's beyond cruel and made worse by the fact that it's usually me who takes charge and brings all the elements of contentment together instead of cracking it open, like a rotten egg with all the hopelessness in my head spilling out and spoiling everything.

We used to share everything and life was so full of fun, excitement, ambition, success and then suddenly we all cried alone, separated by my hopelessness. All communication ceased and I could hardly bare to look anyone in the eye because of the shame I felt. I think my psyche decided that it had grafted enough; my subconscious had given up so there was nothing left. My brain separated itself from my body and no longer functioned as part of my me but now and again I would force it to work and try to focus on simple things, like what day it was or what I had done the night before.

"How did that make you feel?"

I felt as if I was no longer in control of my actions or my thoughts because something else had taken over I couldn't do fundamental things, like wash my face or even make a cup of tea. Water, kettle, cup, sugar, teabag, were too much to cope with, so without the most basic functionality I simply went back to bed. Everything went into slow motion. Lying in that room watching the sun rise then closing my eyes to the brightness of it was exhausting and zapped me of every ounce of will I mustered to try and exist.

After what seemed like an eternity I'd look at my phone to see how much time had passed to realise it was still round one of twenty-four, the same hour that it took for my arms to ache from clutching my compliant pillow. Sometimes I could hear the sound of crying in another room and the pounding of a heart beating like a time bomb, ticking away, only to recognize it as my own. Waiting in the dark 'til everyone was asleep so I could get up and seek some secret remedy, anything that would numb my nothingness.

I needed something to help me sleep, knock myself out or I would lie awake and listen to the day start without me and again, curl up, crying, wishing I knew what to do. I would have been as well hitting myself over the head with a bottle as it would have had the exact same effect on me. Do you know that alcohol is involved in around two thirds of suicide attempts, Tam? Of course you do 'cause that's your job; must be fucking depressing. Tam, are you awake. You reminded me of a budgie we had once. It used to sleep with its eyes open too.

Even having a shower became a monstrous task, so I didn't bother. My skin began to smell Tam and it reminded me of when someone dies and there is that pungent, sickly odour disguised by the stinging, sharp scent of lilies. But there were no lilies or rose petals to mask the smell or transform me from the corpse that I'd become back into the marvel that I'd been. There were no mourners or songs or prayers because I wasn't dead - not yet.

So, I suppose everyone bothered less with me because it had come to the point where there was nothing that anyone could do. They were powerless in their dejection. I glimpsed my beautiful daughter's red, ringed eyes; her once chatty mouth which was now still, silent and sad. I acknowledged her swollen, sorry lips and I offered no mother's kiss or reassurance. All I provided was fear, concern and dread to everyone who loved me. How could I cause them such grief when before I had showered them with unconditional love and positive energy? I had to do something about it!

"Tell me more about this?"

Yes, of course Tam but I don't actually mind if you zone out, might be better if you do because, as I said before, I don't want to drive you nuts.

Anyway, since you asked, one morning I woke from one of my drunken or chemically induced sleeps and I went downstairs slowly, making sure that everyone had gone out. I went into the back room and put the television on. Little did I know that breakfast television was about to become my knight in shining armour.

Richard and Judy were on, I know Tam, that's how bad it got

Rampant Richard and Jittery Judy. They were interviewing a guest and discussing mental health issues and post-natal depression. Although my daughters were in their late teens I related completely to what they were saying and knew I needed help. They seemed to be talking directly to me and I felt as if they could see me in my bathrobe, with unkempt hair and as they were talking I imagined they could smell me and I felt ashamed. Can you have post-natal depression for 30 years Tam? Maybe that's what's wrong with me. Postpartum!

Anyway, I went to the computer and Googled depression and the first thing that I found out was that you could do a course in Mental Health First Aid training. It is a bit like normal First Aid although you don't just stick on a plaster or perform the *Heineken Manoeuvre*. There's a lot more to it than that. They teach you how to look out for people like myself who might have come to the end of Sanity Row. Maybe I could even begin to cut out the middle man, like yourself Tam and do what everyone had been suggesting and literally 'pull *myself* together' or 'sort *myself* out' and actually thought of starting my own business. 'Post-Partum Incorporated'. Don't you be stealing that idea now Tam!

Then again, I thought, I could learn those skills and put them to good use by recognising despair in others and taking appropriate action. Tam, I honestly thought about using my illness as a super power and envisaged myself patrolling the city and dedicating myself to saving people from themselves. That's bonkers eh Tam?

I envisaged myself Policing bridges and railway tracks, swooping down, at that crucial moment, to save someone's anaesthetized soul from oblivion. I even thought of calling myself Psyche Prowler I could have made a difference but instead, I simply phoned the doctor and he referred me to you and so I've put those plans on hold for the minute and here I am in your hands *Supertam*. Show me your superpower Tam. What exactly is? What the fuck is it you're paid to do? Sitting there fucking staring at me for hours on end. I was willing to go out there and risk life and limb to help people and what do you do sit and gawp at me sitting her on a chair talking pure shite? I would have been a super hero and what are you? A gawper, that's what you are, a gawper, fuck sake. I'm tired!

By the way Tam, what do you get when you take the alcohol out of a fruitcake?

Still a fruitcake!

"Tell Me About Your Childhood!"

My childhood was fine, filled with fighting and Lanliq Wine. In case you don't know Tam it was to the 50s what Buckfast is now, not that you'd know about Buckfast either, wearing your cords and that. The auld yins in our family used to make 'cocktails' with Lannie, as it was called, and hair lacquer, made your hair stand on end that did. Lethal little bastards they were too. The cocktails not the auld yins. By the way that means the elder members of the family in case you're not up to speed with the East End Lingo Tam. Have you ever drunk Lannie or Buckie Tam, no, I bet you like a wee Prosecco? Not that I'm saying you wouldn't like a pint with the boys, it's just the way you sort of hold your pen, as if it's heavy. Can't imagine you with a big, dimple jug full of heavy beer or ale. Not sure it would suit you at all.

"What is your first memory of childhood?"

One of my first memories was of drinking was Babycham, at a party and everything was really sparkly and delicious. The party was to celebrate my parents' twenty-fifth anniversary. Not of marriage though - they had only been married for twelve years - but of separating and then getting together for the twenty fifth time. The most important thing to me was that we were a family again and everything was nearly perfect, 'till they opened the twenty fifth bottle that is.

"Do you have a Happy memory to share?'

I have a fond memory of us living with my grandparents in the country (Hamilton, twenty minutes from Glasgow) and my Grandpa working at the Palace coal mine. He used to come in all covered in soot and would sing Al Jolson songs to us before he went in for a bath. You wouldn't get away with that now eh? The darkie police would come for you. Is it OK to say darkie? After he had his dinner he would tell us funny stories and we would laugh our heads off. He always seemed really interested in what we had been doing while he was at work. There was always so much to do there and our days were filled with fun and fresh air.

"What were those mornings Like?"

We'd run out early in the morning and down past the river and stay out all day in the sunshine until we were too tired to eat the piping hot dinner waiting for us on our return. The long, sunny days were spent making daisy chains and eating berries from the hedgerows that lined the path to the farm where the farmer would invite us in and give us eggs to take home in a white cotton napkin which we would return to him the next day. ...Or was that 'Little House on the Prairie'? My memory is a bit mangled.

"Try to remember what it was like."

The lambing season was one of the most exciting times and the farmer would sometimes let us help. Well, it was actually only once but I'll never forget it, they never let us near the farm again after that time. I loved the lambs, they were absolutely gorgeous and with the help of my grandpa we even made up some names for them like Lammy, Scrummy, Minty and Delicious. He liked lambs too and everything was great, until he invented a new game for us, then we got into terrible trouble.

He explained to us how the farmer didn't really love the lambs in the same way that we did and he certainly wouldn't miss one of them, because to him they were all the same. He hadn't even given them names. I knew exactly what he meant because sometimes I could even tell Minty from Scrummy and I loved them both very much. He explained the rules to us and we were going to start to play it the very next day. I could hardly sleep with the excitement of it all and imagined the rest of my life being filled with joy and farmyard enchantment, just like it was 'On the Banks of Plum Creek'.

It was going to be great, like going to the funfair and then taking your favourite ride home with you. About teatime the next day we were to wait until the farmer wasn't looking and widen the wires at the bottom end of the field near the road. One of us would entice a little lamb and encourage it to come through the fence. I was picked because I was the smallest. My job was to get the wee lamb through the hole in the fence and take it up the back lane while my sister and two brothers skipped past the farmer waving and skipping.

"Why do you think they picked you?"

Because I was the smallest. I was put in charge of 'fence-gate', so off I went to where all the sheep and lambs were congregated. As I tried to loosen the wire one of the posts came right out of the ground, leaving a big, gaping hole in the fence. I thought this was great as it would make it easier for the wee lamb to get through. When the others arrived we began trying to lure Mint but we hadn't taken into account that lambs were only interested in mother's milk. They were not, at all, enamoured with the lollipops we had brought as bait. Also, every time one of them came near us all the others followed and we had to chase them back.

After what seemed like hours of toing and froing we decided to go home and leave them alone. We were all very tired by this time and it was starting to get dark so we headed down the main road towards the house. Then suddenly, as if we were dreaming, we heard bleating and turned to see all the sheep, wagging their tails, behind us. We had no clue, what to do, so we started to run, hoping that they would get lost and we would not get the blame.

"Did you get the blame?"

Sort of. When we got back to the house and told them what had happened, my grandma was furious and took my Grandpa through to the kitchen and we could hear them fighting. By this time, we knew that things were very serious because we had been left sitting in the parlour, which smelt like an old tomb by the way Tam, and we were hardly ever allowed in there. They were bawling and shouting about sheep and lambs and someone getting hung and we were all terrified we were going to be executed.

When the police arrived with the farmer we were made to stand in front of them in the grim room and apologise. We explained that we had been mistaken and said that our interpretation of a bedtime story was completely incorrect and that we had been very stupid to take what my Grandpa had said literally. So, what had started with a sparkling Perry and a bedtime story ended in a nightmare of a hangover with the shake of a lamb's tale.

"Where was your Dad at this point?"

He was away working because money and food, especially fresh lamb, was in short supply my Grandpa got my Dad a job down the pit but he only went for two days. He couldn't stand the dirt in his hair and under his nails and before we knew it he was off again to get work somewhere else. He fancied himself as a boxing promoter and so he left us there to follow his dream and said he would come back for us when he had 'made it'. My Mum hardly came out of her room after that and when she did it was only to fight with my Granny and we were off, back to the big city.

It wasn't long before we were celebrating again. My Dad turned up with a big smile, a pocketful of money and a bag that tinkled with sparkling, party water. He was full of stories about his new venture and how he was going to be the manager of the next world champion. Part of his 'job' involved spending time in his office which was the snug in one of the local pubs and he would go there every night to do his business. One night my mum thought she would surprise him and go round there for a drink. We never saw her for months after that.

"Where did she go?"

Seemingly she turned up at The Star and asked for my Dad. The landlord thought she was one of Pat's 'girls' and gave her the address of a house around the corner where he was doing 'business'. She got there and slowly walked up the stairs to the flat. The door was open. It was very noisy and the hall was filled with smoke and there was a strong stench of Tabu and alcohol. As if in a trance, she slowly wafted from room to room taking in scenes of debauchery which she could not make any connection with. She was sure there had been some mistake until she was stopped in her tracks by what was right in front of her.

There he was, my Dad, drink in hand, being straddled by a semi-naked woman in a room full of strangers. She felt disengaged and sensed that her life, as she knew it, was about to come to an end. Her heart had burst wide open for all to see and all she felt was hatred because everything she had begun to cherish and hope for was threatened. Suddenly it was as if an electric charge surged through her body and she lifted a bottle form a nearby table, smashed it against the fireplace and lunged towards him and plunged it into his head.

All we were told at the time was that she was not well and would be in hospital for a while but we couldn't go to see her because it was too far away. My Dad tried to look after us but he was not very skilled. Should have stuck to boxing really. He went out for a pint and it was a couple of weeks before the authorities were informed and we were taken from the house to 'places of safety'. My brothers went to a 'lovely big house' by the seaside and my sister and I were packed off to a 'boarding' school. It was about three months before we saw my mother again and my dad had disappeared completely off the face of responsibility.

"Did you see him again?"

When my mother died he came back to live near me but he had been away for so long and we had to get to know each other all over again. At first, when we sat together, he would scarcely speak and all he did was weep and say over and over again how sorry he was for not being there when we were young. His hair was snow white, like a new-born lamb, the same as my mother's had been before she died and as I stroked his head he would curl up and fall asleep like little

Tom Dacre.   From there we began to sweep away the dusty memories of the past and I thanked him for giving me the Babycham that had made my childhood sparkle.   Do you like fresh meat Tam, bet you do!

"How is your general health?"

I've never really had problems with my health and I've only been in hospital to have my children well, until now. No wait, I've just remembered, there was this one time when I fell in the bathroom. Don't remember much about it. Went for a pee, then bang, nothing, nada. It was scary. I ended up in hospital. Imagine that? Go to the toilet and then end up in a hospital bed, drips, needles, doctors, the whole shah-bang!

You see, I was experiencing a really bad period. You know, menstrual, not time in my life or anything like that. Do you know what I mean am? This is a bit embarrassing. Are you okay with me talking about this Tam? I would never have spoken about anything like this to my dad or any male, family members. In fact, throughout my whole life, my dad never even farted in front of us...imagine that, nearly fifty year sans never even a whiff of a fart, amazing. He would have died first or held it in for so long that he would have farted out of his eye.

I think the real reason men don't like to talk about these things is because they are scared. It's always been the same, even in the old days, I sound like a fucking historian don't I Tam. Did you know that women in Celtic culture were held in very high regard and were totally in control of their own lives? Virginity was actually frowned upon as it was not productive and one of the most important positions in society was the child-churning Priestess; red headed ones especially because they were noted as having special healing and reproductive abilities and, because of this, were revered by all and sundry. So Tam, if we take into account *my* flaming, red hair and menstrual state at the moment then men must be shit scared of *me*.

I might change my name to Boadicea.

I'm sure I conceived daughter number one on Christmas day. Had I lived in the Celtic era I would have been afforded remarkable importance. Also, the Druids thought holly was the symbol of blood and ivy represented semen. So, I would have been held in such high esteem that nothing I did would have been questioned. Not even the fact that I was found naked, during the night, on my exercise bike. It would have been considered absolutely okay. Not one person would have deemed it strange and I would not be sitting here with you know. I would have gotten away with murder never mind a static, bare, bike ride.

"So, you were telling me about the period...sorry, time...?"

That's right, where was I? Oh yes, my periods have recently become a bit of a problem, really heavy and extremely debilitating. Simply going to do a bit of shopping is becoming a problem. Just the other day I was standing in the butchers waiting to buy some steak and whoosh! Now, that was very awkward but I just had to get on with it. Although it did put me right off the idea of eating steak and I bought some chicken fillets instead. Do you know that they can measure your menstrual blood? Well, women's, obviously, not yours. Are you okay Tam? You seem to have gone a bit pale? Don't you just hate that when the blood just rushes from one part of your body to another?

Anyway, on my next visit to the hospital the doctor said that he would like to check how much blood I was losing each month. They can actually do that Tam, extract the blood, from the tampons and towels. Isn't that amazing? You would think they would just know what the weight of the protection was and then deduct that from the 'used' weight but they have to allow for evaporation and all sorts of other eventualities. Isn't that awfully clever? Doctors and scientists are really amazing aren't they? I'm sure you're amazing at something as well Tam and someday I might even find out what it is!

Anyway, what they expected me to do was to conserve all the used pads and 'plugs' and take them with me on my next visit. Or, I could simply hand them in to the reception desk with a label on them. Not on each individual piece of protection you understand, but, in a sealed bag, with the label on the outside. Are you following me Tam? I didn't have to tag every single item; that would be disgusting; my name went on the outside of the pack. It would have been funny though, giving each of them a name. Bloody Nora, Polly Plasma and Bobby Fluid they would have been good names. Then some poor soul has the job of taking them out of the bag, placing them into a solution which extracts all the fluid and then, hey presto, it's all ready to be measured.

Imagine doing that for eight hours a day, five days a week? You're lucky all you have to do is listen to me. They never talk about jobs like that when you visit the careers' office at school, do they? Not the sort of job where you would take the work home with you is it? Imagine:

> *"Hello dear, just brought some work home with me from the office. Could you get me a large Le Creuset and fire up the Aga?"*

The instructions made it all sound so easy and you would think that it would be but it wasn't that straightforward at all. It was some sort of trial they were doing at the time but I never actually got the chance to take part in it, which was disappointing really. You see, I worked in a department store at the time and we had to sign in and out at the security office and sometimes they had 'on the spot' bag checks. Could you fucking imagine it? I tried to slip them out once but I was sweating and shaking and couldn't even look the security guy in the eye and I felt sure he would stop me the next day and I was bloody right. They very next evening, just as I was leaving, the security guard stopped me and asked to look in my bag. Thank the lord I'd had the forethought to dispatch the offenders into the disposal unit. So nothing awkward was found in my bag. No stolen goods, or manky pads. It made me wonder what would have happened if they had found them, what would have been more serious, carrying offensive sanitary protection or stealing stock? What could they have charged me with anyway, theft or being a bloody nuisance?

"Tell me about your parents"

Both dead!

They were separated most of the time but they always loved one another. They couldn't live with together and were hopelessly chaotic when apart. My mother was the youngest of four children and was very spoilt. She didn't have a clue about looking after children or how to manage money. When she got it, she spent it, without a thought for tomorrow. It was either a famine or a feast with nothing in the middle. We did have lots of good times but for every one of them there were heart-breaking episodes that I can't bear to think about. I'm tired Tam can we have a wee break?

"Tell me about your Dad."

You are fucking relentless. O.K, I'll tell you about my Dad and unlike you he was very dapper and got his suits made for him, by a 'master tailor', so there. Never in my life did I see him wearing any tartan shirts or ugly, fucking, cord trousers. Right up until he died he had never bought a suit off the peg; nothing. He had loads of hats and when he died he wanted all his clothes to be taken to a pub in Hamilton to be given away to guys who 'never had anything', as he put it. Wasn't that generous? He loved going into that pub and was such a show off. Even when he didn't have two pennies to rub together he always looked a million dollars and was always full of his own importance. You're a bit like him in that respect Tam. Those old guys were so grateful and the irony was that some of them couldn't even remember who he was. He would have hated that.

My Mum used to go on about 'him and his fancy clothes' but she loved it when he turned up and took her out. She would get all dolled up and she would always make sure they had a substantial 'carry out' for when they got back to the house. Very proactive she was, especially where drink was concerned. No food in the house but a drink for after a night out was essential. We would be starving and he would turn up, buy fish and chips and off they'd go to the pub. When it got near to closing time we would all hide under the bedclothes or a pile of coats because we knew it would all end in tears.

Even when he was telling us he loved us it was torture. He would line us up against the wall and lift our chins up to look at him and ask. I loved them both but when drink was involved they were psychopaths.

> *"How much do you love me? Do you want me to come back? I love you all more than anything else in the world. I think about you all the time. I love your mother too; there will never be anyone else for me. How much do you love me? I love your mum. There's never been anyone else. Look at me when I'm talking to you. Do you not want to listen? Is that what it is? Am I boring you? Ungrateful wee bastards!"*

One morning I got up and my jaw was bruised and my neck ached because he had lifted my head up so much in order to tell me how much he loved me. He had the bloody cheek to ask me what had happened to me. *'You happened'* is what I wanted to scream at him. I've read all this shit about how some children feel as if they're to blame; in some way they deserve it but I never felt like that. The two of them were useless. I just wanted to get away, as far away as I possibly could, even if it meant…well I was too young to understand what dying meant but anything seemed preferable to that.

Some nights we stood there for what seemed like hours, in the freezing cold, like tiny soldiers, upright and alert in our vests and pants. The boys would be crying and we'd shake and shiver. My brothers were only three and four years old at the time and we would be called to attention for what seemed like an eternity. Abduction for use in combat might have been preferable to the battle we had to face on a Saturday night. At least that way we would have had proper food and some decent clothes and would get to sleep at a reasonable hour. Maybe even a remedy to block out the reality. Oh, and a gun, a gun would have been good. I would have shot the bastard or turned it on myself. What? Not sure, I might have been about seven or eight.

After a couple of days, he would leave again and my Mum would be dead sad and take to her bed for days on end. She did, however, make sure he gave her money before he left or she would threaten to phone the police. She would cry and drink for days and tell us how much she loved him and how there would never be anyone else. I remember once looking her in her room for about two days. I thought I could save her. I tied a rope from the door handle to the banister so that she couldn't get out for more drink. My plan was to let her sleep it off and then I'd make some 'home made', Bachelors actually but she used to tell us she'd been up all night making it and thought we didn't know. Soup, I thought that would fix her, help with her recovery. It was the impression I got from their adverts, that soup sorted everything. However, it didn't quite go to plan. Nothing ever went to plan because there was none.

"Where were you living at this time?"

We lived in The Gorbals at the time, on the main road called Crown Street. On the first day of my parenting *project* I opened the door a couple of times to check if she was OK then took her in some dinner. She told me how sorry she was and that she would sort herself out. She told me she was very tired and wanted to go back to sleep and asked if I would let her rest for a couple of hours. Later that night though, I heard singing and when I went into the room, there she was, drunk as a skunk, with a bottle of vodka, absolutely blootered. It was genius, pure genius!

You see Tam, her room faced onto the road and she'd called to someone from the window and thrown over some money and had asked them to go to the off-sales for her. When the guy came back with the carry-out she lowered her shopping bag, on a string, and then hoisted it up and voila, she poured it into a teacup, tried to control the shakes, get the cup to her lips and gulp! That's what she did, and her recovery was remarkable. Before I knew it she was up and about and things were back to normal. All my hard work gone in 75cl. of vodka.

We laughed about it later when I joined her and had a wee glass myself. She was very persuasive like that. Sometimes, when they were all drinking, they made me feel daft and told me that I was 'a boring, wee bastard', so it was easier to fit in if I joined them. So that's what I did. I joined in. I did so to the point that it began to seem like the right thing to do. The only problem Tam was that I was the only person working so I had to pay for the party and what I earned was never enough. I was at college and had two jobs but I never seemed to have any money. In the end I decided to leave the college course I was doing and go to work full-time so I could keep the party going and the drink flowing.

"Were they ever happy together?"

Yes, sometimes; although I can't actually think of a time right now, except maybe when they were drunk and they would sing to each other. They had songs for each other, my Mum and Dad and you would think it would be romantic but their recitals were more like assaults than serenades. My Dad's song was Mario Lanza's 'Because You're Mine' and we used to have such a laugh because his singing was bad at the best of times but when he was drunk it was hilarious. He be sitting there, on the only, comfy chair, holding a half bottle of whisky and taking a swig after every couple of lines. I often wondered whether he was singing to the bottle or to her because half the time she was already in a drink induced coma. He would be chanting and he so engrossed in his deliciously, potent, amber friend that he didn't even notice. She could have died, right there in front of him and he'd be totally unaware.

Then if and when she eventually woke up she would burst into a horrific rendition of:

> *"I used to walk with you, along the avenue;*
> *our hearts were carefree and gay. Somehow I*
> *knew I'd lose you. Somewhere along the way."*

Who was it that sung that Tam? Oh, I know, Nat King Cole.

In the years before my Dad died he played that record every day, it used to drive me mad. I know all the words; it's embedded in my brain. If I hear it on the radio, I have to switch off. My brain, the radio, everything. It sends me into a spiral like Dante's inferno till I'm deep in the depth of Lucifer and wonder what happened to God's plan for human happiness!

How could two people who loved each other so much not have the strength to stay together? I just don't get it. He never had another woman - well, he had women, but he never lived with anyone else and neither did she. Why could they not, just, fix things, for our sake? It was always about them, always. They were both totally self-absorbed.

Not sure if I said before but I was his favourite, which was a bit of a nightmare because he kept trying to snatch me. That sounds rude doesn't it, snatch me! Every time they separated he would turn up and hover about the school and try to take me away with him. This was the *non-preferred* kind of snatching to Hamilton, not as I would have liked; to be back in the children's home or to be abducted and forced to become a soldier. Final destination: granny's house. A war zone in Uganda would have been preferable to staying with her Majesty. God help me and save me, she was an old reptile; I'm named after her you know? She used to proffer her cheek for a kiss whilst looking the other way and holding a hanky over her nose. I hated the feel of her dry, scaly skin and felt as if I was walking on egg-shells when she came close. She was a cold-blooded old bastard and I'm called after her.

On another 'apprehension' day I met my dad on the road just down from the school, on the corner of Dalmarnock Road and Dunn Street. There was a wee bookie's shop on the corner and about six men were standing outside. My dad approached me and asked if I wanted to go for dinner to Grand-mama's house. There was absolutely no way I was heading there with him; even if it did mean I got fresh food on the table and milky porridge in the morning, fuck that I thought but how would I get out of it and then I came up with a genius plan!

As soon as he come over to me I started to scream and shout and some of the men came across the road and asked me if I was okay? They looked like three big bears, enormous they were and rough as anything. My dad said everything was fine and explained who he was, at which point I started to cry and said I'd never seen him before in my life. I was really good at crying on demand and the men believed me and dealt with the situation in the only way they knew how. As one of the men pulled me away my dad got his hat knocked off and was getting his head kicked in, I didn't expect him to get hurt and immediately, sort of, regretted my spontaneous action plan.

Meanwhile one of the men took me home and when he heard me telling my mum what I had just done to my dad he went mental and called me a 'stupid little bastard' and ran back up the road to try and save him from certain disability. Those men took no prisoners you know. My mum was dead proud of me though and that night and we had a great laugh telling all the neighbours. They even had a party in my honour to celebrate.

You see Tam, I was well aware of what to do if someone approached me because a few weeks before I'd had a very lucky escape. This man had approached me while I was playing in the street and asked me to go for a loaf of bread for him and I said 'of course I would'. We used to go to the corner shop for the neighbours all the time and they would give us money to buy sweeties. Sometimes old Robert downstairs would call me and ask me to go into his house and make him a cup of tea. One time I went in and he had shit in the sink and it was all over the tap. I was nearly sick. No amount of money was worth that. Not even enough money for a bag of chips was worth putting up with that crap.

Anyway, this guy was different, not smelly at all and very polite. It was a bit strange because he told me that he knew a shop where the bread was cheaper and he would go with me. I did think it was odd but I was desperate for some Highland Toffee, so I went anyway. As we got further down the road he pointed to a derelict building and said the shop was just on the other side of it. Well, I knew that was a lie because, luckily for me, my family had been evicted from that, very, same building just a couple of weeks before so I knew that the shop had been closed down.

I panicked and started to scream and shout and he grabbed me by the pixie. That's nothing rude either by the way, it was a knitted hat. I managed to break his grasp although my pixie did get torn in the ensuing struggle to get free. I ran all the way back to the street and continued to play with my friends. We used to use chalk to draw houses on the pavement. My living rooms were always the most beautiful. Mine usually had a sofa, television and on the table I would draw lovely plates, teacups and saucers. That was the kind of table that I would have in my house when I was older. All nice and proper and I could invite people who talked polite and were posh, like the bread man, over for tea.

"What happened with the bread man?"

Oh, yes, of course, later, when my mum asked how my hat had got torn I told her about the man and the cheap bread; she went mental and called on all the neighbours. The men grabbed hammers, 'chibs' and other weapons of child protection then left to investigate the old tenement flats. Although there was no-one there at the time, in one of the top floor houses they found lots of empty bottles and a dirty, old mattress. It looked as if there'd been someone staying there. They waited for ages in silence but they did not find anyone and my mum reluctantly went and reported it to the police.

Just a week after the 'cheap bread' incident, a girl went missing. The whole city seemed to be searching for her and it was all everyone talked about. They found her body three weeks later. The little soul had been stuffed into a cupboard down in a disused railway station. She had been brutally raped and her body was covered in knitting needle punctures. They never did find the person who did it.

So, there was no more playing in the street for a while after that and we were only able to go to the shops for the neighbours if someone was with us. My mum and dad got back together for a while. As for me, no real harm was done as it was only my pixie that got damaged and someone could always knit me another one, couldn't they?

"Have you been experiencing mood swings?"

No…

Fuck Off!

"How are you feeling today?"

Oh my God Tam, I'm feeling really energetic this morning so, watch out, hang on to your corduroys. Some days I just can't fit enough in and I'm like a pure maniac. It's fantastic how much you can get done in one day. I remember one day after one of my quieter episodes I was at the dentist for nine, the print shop at ten, hairdressers at eleven and then had my feet done by twelve. I spent a hundred quid into the bargain. That's not including the dentist, because that might cost anything up to three hundred. I've not had the bill for that yet.

By twelve o'clock my head was spinning and I realised that I hadn't eaten since I'd had my cereal at seven thirty. I sped off to the supermarket to buy some fuel. Not a good idea. Have you ever done that, gone food shopping when you are starving? No? Well, I bought the biggest pile of junk ever. I wanted everything. I filled a trolley with enough ingredients to make lasagne, chilli, meatballs, curry, stew and a ready-made haggis, because the real stuff takes two hours to heat through, by the way. No time for that.

Although some of the best dishes, like stew and curry...oh and homemade soup are best eaten the next day aren't they? Another thing is that if you do cook the night before, you might not feel like eating that particular thing the next day. Or you might be too busy, or not go home at all and go out for dinner instead. It is important though to try and eat healthily to keep your stamina up isn't it Tam? I can tell just by looking at you that fast food is your friend and you like to top up without too much effort, eh Tam? Och, put a smile on yer face, I'm only joking you. You're not that fat although I do think you would suit tailored trousers better because those ones are a bit bulky!

Goodness, when you think about it life is a cycle of shopping, cooking, thinking about what to have next and snacking in between. It's a wonder we have time to use up any energy doing challenging activities at all. I wonder how many calories we burn up while we are eating. Wouldn't it be strange if eating helped you lose weight in your face because of all the chewing? All the really fat people would have tiny faces then wouldn't they?

Imagine if your head got smaller the fatter you got. I suppose if you got really, really fat then your head would be out of proportion anyway. That would be the opposite of those anorexic looking models who hold their heads at an angle because they are too heavy for their skinny necks to hold up. Also, I wonder if twins shared their energy one would be fat with a sunny disposition and the other skinny and all dull and miserable. Do you know that they say that one twin is usually gay and the other one is left handed? Did you know that Tam? I don't know exactly who said it but it makes some sense if the DNA is split down the middle. So really, if you think about it, they wouldn't be the same at all. I need to find out more about that. My goodness my mind is working overtime today. I'm starving.

Roasted cheese, that's what I fancy, right now. Or is it toasted? Roasted or toasted, I'm not sure but you make it under the grill and it is far too easy to eat. I could eat about six slices in one go. It's more a snack than a proper meal though. I'm usually in such a hurry to eat it I burn my tongue. I can scoff it in the time it takes to make a cup of coffee. Then I'm looking for something to eat with the coffee. What did I actually make yesterday? Don't remember. What did you ask me again?

What? Sorry, I'm still thinking about the toasted-roasted thing and I could be mixed up because when I was young the grill on the cooker was at eye level and now my grill is in the top of the oven. Tam, you're not getting it are you? You look a bit confused but the fact is that things are toasted under the grill and roasted in the oven.

Tam, could you imagine asking someone to make toasted cheese and they put it straight into a toaster. That would be so funny. Don't you think so Tam? I do. I know people who are that stupid. One of my friends made biscuits without using flour. No, wait a minute... I think that was me.

Chocolate and coffee is a lethal combination for a wee energy boost isn't it? One time I knocked back so much I had a twitch for three days and lost about a stone and a half in weight. Well maybe not that much but I was a lot speedier and could hardly catch a breath so it's bound to have been more than a couple of pounds.

Fast food is really bad for you, but sometimes, it's just what the doctor ordered. Have you ever done that Tam? Given a prescription for fast food? Instead of the chemist: MacDonald's! If I go to McD's then I'm finished and out in about, maybe, ten minutes. There have been times though when I've got back into the car and thought 'I need something to eat' and have completely forgotten that I have just had something.

Other times Tam I'm so hungry that I start to shake and can't think a straight thought. My mind scrambles and it's as if my brain is going to explode. I also feel like that when I drink espresso. When I've got lots to do and need a helping hand, that's what I drink, espresso.

It's like, BOOM! An instant hit. Fantastic!

I'm planning on doing a five kilometre run soon. My daughter and I are doing it together. Although I'll probably hold her back as she is much fitter than me. We did ask my other daughter if she wanted to do it with us but she's busy that day. She did it before and finished in twenty-three minutes. That was good because it was her first time. I suppose the time it takes you to finish depends on lots of different factors. Fitness, what you've eaten, sleep and well, other stuff.

Going along to the Race for Life is a great day out. It's supposed to be exclusively for women but we saw two 'women' who were clearly not. They were obviously men but they must have signed up in someone else's name. Also, they were wearing high heels and women would never be that stupid.

It did put the officials on the spot as they were too embarrassed to approach them and say anything. On the other hand, maybe they weren't men at all and were really, ugly women. Funny that isn't it Tam, that a guy, dressed as a woman, can look unattractive but as himself looks okay. I think you might look good in drag Tam. Do you think drag queens ever take make-up classes? Have you ever dressed up as a woman Tam?

"Could you concentrate on how you feel at the moment."

Well, ok, I always dress as a woman and can wake up, have a shower, dry my hair and have my make-up done in less than forty-five minutes, or, half an hour at a push. If I go swimming though it takes me longer to get ready but I think it's because of the changing rooms and the way they are set up. I mean, at home we have a ritual don't we? Everything is in its place and all that, but when we are in another setting it's more challenging.

Know what I can't stand Tam? Staying at someone else's house. Waking in the morning, desperate to get up but there is not a sound and you just lie there waiting for some action. Have you ever woken up and then drifted back to sleep and had a dream that you get ready and then wake up and have to do it all again? I hate that.

I love swimming and sometimes when I go to the local baths I can do sixty lengths in about forty minutes. I remember one time doing my quota in twenty-five minutes and thought I would stay and do another twenty lengths, to get my money's worth. Eventually, when I stepped out of the pool I fell flat on my face and burst my nose. The guards had to come and lift me to the changing rooms because I had lost the feeling in my legs.

Sometimes it doesn't do, to do too much no matter how energetic you feel does it Tam? Dogs are funny aren't they? Mine can be out for the count. Sound, as if she's dead. Then I say one word and she is hyper. Not just any word by the way. It's PARK. I have to say 'PARK' to get her attention. I often say it just to get her reaction. That's cruel isn't it? My daughter says it's not the word but the way I say it that gets her going. The dog that is, not my daughter.

Sometimes, when she's asleep, she does that thing. Do you know the thing I mean? They lie on their side and look as if they are running and not going anywhere? That must be exhausting. Imagine waking up having been for a big sprint across a limitless expanse of land and then some daft bastard puts a lead on you and takes you for a real walk. I would hate that. It must be a relief for her when I've been swimming and I only take her out for two minutes.

What? No, I was talking about the dog. Did you think I meant my daughter? That's too funny. Although, she would kill me for telling anyone this, she sucks her tongue in her sleep thinking it is a dummy, you know, a soother. Some mornings she has to take pain killers because the pain in her jaw is so bad. She's twenty-nine now and I still think that maybe I took the soother away from her too soon. Dreams can be very vivid can't they Tam?

"What is your favourite time of day?"

Mornings used to be my best time and I would spring out of bed as soon as I woke up but it's different now. There are days when I can barely open my eyes and it's an effort to pull myself out of bed. On those days the only plan I have is to sit by the window and watch the world go slowly by. I could sit for hours, days sometimes, just staring, at the clouds, waltzing past, moving on to the next party in heaven. Dancing clouds gathering to celebrate, having nothing to do but wait to rain down on us, downpours that went on for seconds, minutes, hours, days, weeks, months.

Sometimes, imagining I'm up there with them, hovering above the world, with no worries or care, was all I could manage. Feelings of weightlessness and emptiness overwhelmed me and I pictured myself floating away, trying my damned not to move, letting the wind take control so that nature took me on its course.

For a while I had this recurring dream where I'd get up very early in the morning and walk for miles over sand dunes to the edge of the sea. I'd then carefully place my shoes at the edge of the water before treading slowly towards the rise. The tide then carried me out and the noise of the waves whooshed over my head as I am sent into a smiling sleep where my body is so relaxed that I feel nothing. Not even the summery, shroud of silken sanity that everyone thinks has returned. Like a dream within a dream.

Then suddenly, the tide turns and I'm facing downwards, looking at the landscape of my life and I want to go back. Then I see him, sobbing on the beach, I can't see his face but I know he's crying for what he's lost. He`s holding what he had left of me. My remains are embedded into the leather and he wipes his tears on them, mixing part of him with what was left of me. I try to call out and get back but it's too late and the wind whips me back and I'm abruptly entombed in a chilling cask and can't even move my eyes.

Some dreams are exhausting aren't they Tam?

I'm quite tired now; can we stop there for the day?

"Do you have any regrets?"

Well, if you think of the exact definition of the word then *my life* has been, literally regretful. Most of what I have felt for the past twenty years is a sense of loss, sorrow, anguish, grief and sadness due to episodes out with my control. No-one can help you when your heart aches. That's something you have to deal with all on your own. Even the doctors, no matter how gifted and caring they are, can't do anything about a broken heart.

Maybe someday they'll come up with something like a pill or an antidote. They could call it something like 'Wallow while you Swallow' or 'Consume when you're in Gloom'. You never know there might come a day when they can go right inside you and fix this, so easily broken, organ. There could be special surgeons called heart menders and they could make lots of money from lonely, lost and vulnerable people. The NHS could make a few bob from that. You should put that forward at your next meeting Tam.

The only thing I can think of with some reproach is the time that I wasted trying to save Jesus. What a desecration that turned out to be. I mean, even at the age of five, I had a good idea he was already dead because we 'ate his body and drank his blood' every Sunday at the Sacred Heart chapel. That was a clue in itself that he was no longer with us and even if he was hovering about then he was definitely a bit past his sell by date

Being brought up as a Catholic was very confusing for me Tam because everything seemed so contradictory. We were taught to love Jesus but then, on a Sunday, we became a bunch of cannibalistic vampires eating Jesus. It was terrifying and I used to watch the ladies with their nice hats and fancy coats going up to the altar and drinking from the chalice. They were all prim and proper and then had this contented look on their faces after swigging the Lord's liquid. I can tell you it made my blood surge chillingly through my veins. I thought they were all vampires.

My mum would tell us, from the comfort of her bed, to bring back the order of service to prove that we had been to mass. Then she would read it while my big sister made the breakfast. Even the headmaster at school would scream and shout in the corridors that 'God is everywhere' and could see and hear everything. Jesus; however, seemed to take a break when Mr. Christianity was assaulting children with his leather, weapon of mass, confidence destruction. I suppose, in his mind, he was only doing his job because corporal punishment was embedded into the curriculum. Bloody hypocrites the lot of them! Bet you liked a good whipping Tam?

'Til this day I still feel very nervous using public toilets and always have a sneaky feeling that I'm being watched. As soon as I lock the door I start to sing so that the whoosh of my pee is not heard by any of the neighbouring urinators never mind the 'big man' himself and let's not get started on sex. Swear to God they used to call it 'dirty things'. "You better not be doing dirty things!" my mum would say if I was going out with a boy. I hadn't a fucking clue what she meant. Used to be scared to go on a date in case he shoved me in a puddle or something, or worse still, asked me to mud wrestle. Dirty things indeed.

When I used to pray or go up for communion I always went to the left side of the altar because here was this painting of Jesus on the cross and it hung on a chain that was too long. I would kneel under it and yearn for someone to shorten the chain and straighten up the picture. He, Jesus, looked so uncomfortable; hanging over, as if he was going to be sick and I used to wish that I could rescue him. I spent hours devising ways to break into the church or get behind the altar with a set of tools and fix him. I know he would be very grateful and it would lead to my predisposition to Heaven. The only time I did try to fix him resulted in me being punished by an act of contrition that involved twenty Hail Marys and about a million 'Our Da's' as I liked to call them. The cleaner thought I was trying to steal something and chucked me out when I said I was trying to save Jesus by straightening him up.

My Granny, who was a very sincere and serious Catholic, was really upset with me and I went to stay with her in preparation for my First Holy Communion. She could not believe I had been detained by Religious Rebecca, the cleanser of the interior. These women who clean churches never seem to be married and I think that they are all secretly in love with the priest. She was also quite an unfortunate looking lady who really would have benefited from some facial electrolysis but she seemed happy enough.

I remember one day in my Granny's bedroom practising and I put my veil on with the lovely circle of flowers that she had bought me. I was staring at myself in the mirror and thinking I looked like a film star. I took my rosary out of the box and started to walk up and down watching myself walking towards the dressing table mirror. I imagined everyone in the church watching me and talking about the 'wee minx that tried to steal the chalice'. I would show them and give them something to talk about all right. Wait till they see my performance, I'd think.

They never did get to see it though because my Granny caught me in rehearsals wiggling my bum and singing, 'Come Holy Ghost, cha cha cha......!' in front of the mirror and belted me about fifty times with a wooden cross. I have never seen her so animated. She looked like an athlete with both arms extended horizontally, thrashing away. I saw a whole new side to her that day, I can tell you. She could have been overseeing detention in the local school all by herself judging by the ability she demonstrated while administering her wrath that morning.

Shakespeare said, "Better a little chiding than a great deal of heartbreak". Well, I suppose he was partly right because I don't have much to reproach myself for but his prophesy on the heartbreak was way off. I seem to have had my fair share of both. Anyway, regret is said to be evidence of mental distress and if I admit to that now I'll be in big trouble, eh Tam?

"How do you feel about the church now?"

Well, a couple years ago I had an exam in the Barony Hall in Glasgow and with about an hour to spare I went into the St. Mungo's Museum in Castle Street. It was very peaceful and I was drawn upstairs by the brightness from the large windows. Then, suddenly, there it was, "The Crucifixion" by Salvador Dali. It was much bigger than I remembered but just as beautiful. I laughed quietly to myself when I noticed that it was placed flat against the wall and there *he* was, Jesus, still leaning forward. So really, there was no way on this earth I could have fixed him but who knows, maybe he's watching now and he'll come and try to restore my faith in me? So Maybe I didn't save him but I hope he knows I tried.

"What are your thoughts on love?"

Funny old thing love isn't it Tam? When we first got married my husband couldn't grasp the idea of in-laws and always called my mother his mother-in-love which was utterly charming and I couldn't bring myself to correct him. The idea that his association with her was only because of some regulation or consanguineous connection was abhorrent. He felt very welcome and had a sense of belonging to something where all the components were held together by a bond that went beyond culture and statute. He quite liked a drink too you see.

Anyway if you think about it Tam, when it gets to the point where a couple decide to involve the law, then love might just as well be looking for the nearest window to make its escape. The minute a guy, it is usually the guy, proposes then couples are heading towards an institution that's imposed upon us by the state and should never be entered into lightly. Then throw in the fact that nearly fifty per cent of marriages end in divorce it makes you wonder why people rush into it in the first place. I think the guys rush in because they see it as a way to get their washing done. They get to a certain age and their mothers are like, "This is not on son, I'm getting too old for this, get that burd to do your washing from now on." and the only option is to go for the proposal. Well that was in the old days; girls would never put up with that now. Who does your washing Tam? Obviously it's not a woman, I can tell.

You know when you see a proposal on one of those reality programmes I have to watch it through my finger, it's so cringe worthy. Anyone who says yes to a spontaneous knee bender is usually so embarrassed and want it over-with as quickly as possible they blurt out 'yes' in mortification. I can imagine them running off to the toilet and locking themselves in thinking 'What the fuck just happened?'

Think about what happens to Romeo and Juliet in, what is supposed to be, the greatest love story of all time. Here we have a tale of two poisonous, mental lovers who decide to be together against all the odds. For goodness sake, the families were fighting before they even went on a first date and then they killed themselves as soon as possible after the 'wedding'. If the cracks were showing before they even met the in-loves, then we mortals are farting against thunder thinking it will all be a garden of roses. Also, I've always been very wary of the boy next door types, because, if that relationship doesn't work out then you can't even pretend to be out because he will be able to hear you through the wall. Don't you agree, Tam?

Maybe it should be the other way around and we should be forced to go to court before the marriage actually takes place. Imagine if we had to prove, in a court of law, that we loved someone and would do so until death played its part. It's difficult to think of the kind of evidence that we could offer.

What would you do Tam, if you were asked to show love as evidence in court? Would a judge accept a dog wagging its tail or would he say that the dog is simply performing a task in order to be fed and that conditioning had been used in order to win the case? I'm not saying that a dog is the only thing that would pay you any attention or anything like that. I'm just using it as an example because you are actually not that bad looking and it's quite endearing that you always have fluff and dog hair on your clothes.

Anyway, how would they set a precedent and decide what is acceptable for a long lasting and loving union of two consenting advocates of romance? What if we are so programmed by culture and convention to do what is expected of us that we begin to lose the concept of what true love is all about? It would be interesting to see what would happen if defendants were given a trial period and were ordered to report in every so often in order to inform the authorities of their progress. Would everyone be treated the same or would some people be considered more likely to succeed than others depending on their lifestyle and profession?

Scientists for instance, how would they fare in the scheme of passion related issues. Could they profess to be deeply, madly in love and still retain some professional integrity, or would they have to face a mad science tribunal first? Love is not concrete matter that can be analysed and measured so would they still be supported by the UCS if they decided to declare an undying and eternal attachment to another human being?

Then if they failed, could they then, in the case of a male defendant, argue that they were not of sound mind and it was, in fact, their penis that was the catalyst for such and unsubstantiated emotion? That way they could be absolved of all blame and not be forced to present their guilty sex appendage as a witness. Then again, if they were found guilty would they be charged with obsessive-compulsive disorder and be prescribed mood enhancers and condemned to a life of internet pornography as punishment?

No matter who we are, or what we believe in, the beauty of love is that it is not discriminatory and everyone has the God given right to experience it. Some of the most beautiful examples of effortlessly loving relationships I've come across are between same sex couples. Seeing two people who share the most wonderful, natural and non-judgemental form of attachment is something to be envied. Yet they have fought for the right to have something that is so fundamentally flawed it could turn out to be a poisoned chalice. Maybe we should learn to appreciate love and attraction for what it is rather than suffer a need to conform to an idea of what it should be.

At the end of the day perhaps we should all amalgamate and form big love companies where we have targets, spread sheets and tasks to fulfil. There would be no arguing allowed and success would depend on mutual orgasm and shared household duties. Penalties would be given for lack of attention and underpants would be inspected for skid marks and anyone found guilty would forfeit the right to handle the remote control. At least that way we would be sure of getting to see something on the telly that did not involve sport, or cartoons.

There is a song says that 'love and marriage go together like a horse and carriage' but at the end of the day if someone gave me a horse I would be delighted. Although I live in town I could have it put into stables and go to see it whenever it took my fancy. We could go riding in the open air and I would groom it and tame it so that it obeyed my every command. We'd have a mutual and rewarding relationship with both of us gaining equal pleasure but inhabiting very different environments.

On the other hand, if someone dumped a carriage on my property it would be of hardly any use at all and would simply get in my way. I could sit on it now and again but most of the time it would just take up space, gather dust and I would have to constantly justify my reasons for holding onto it. Then, if I wanted to take it anywhere it would be very difficult to move and it would require so much effort that I would give up and just not bother paying it any attention at all. Believe me; one can be just fine without the other and given the choice, I would much rather have a recreational horse than some dead wood.

"Who inspires you?"

In one of my darkest hours I remember being desperate for some sort of sign, anything that would give me a glimmer of hope or understanding of where my mind was taking me. It was a Saturday night and I decided to get in my car and go to Edinburgh. My beloved aunt was in hospital there and had just been told that she had terminal cancer. They offered treatment that would give her another couple of months and she had refused it. I needed to speak to her and find out why she'd made this decision because there was so much that could be done.

My driving was mechanical because the journey was simply a means and end and a chance to unravel the knot in my head. To understand where she got the strength. When I arrived at the ward the lights were low and there was an unsettling silence. As I approached the bed and kissed her soft cheek she opened her twinkling eyes and recognised me immediately and was not at all surprised that I was there so late at night. It was almost as if she was expecting me and for a while I sat there in her presence comforted by a feeling of serenity and a strange sense of hope and an awareness that everything was going to be fine.

She explained to me that if she had accepted the therapy then her family would be forced to suffer physical changes in her that might make the next chapter of their lives more difficult to endure. The short time they had left together needed to be reflective of all the joyous things they had shared. When it was time to leave them she wanted to be the same person in their eyes so that she could rest contentedly in their memories for the time being. The times they had spent at her table with plates overflowing with lovingly made food should be embedded in their hearts and souls forever more.

When I told her how much I envied her faith she implored me to recognise that I had my family to look after me and that she would never be far away. She promised to watch over me and guide me away from harm. She was so serene and sincere that I could no longer impose my sense of uncertainty on her unyielding belief and contentment. I kissed her for what was to be the last time and left to return home hoping that her goodness and righteousness would follow me and keep me safe until the end of my time.

On the way home blinding tears forced me to stop driving and I pulled into one of the service stations. As I stood outside in the freezing cold, sobbing my heart out I noticed something in the sky coming towards me. It was like a ball of flames suspended in the clear, dark nothingness. It seemed to draw me towards it. Surely it was a sign, meant only for me, to let me know that everything would be fine and I would start to get better. Then I heard voices behind me shouting and saying how amazing it was. I turned and asked one of the women if it was the flame she was talking about? She told me it was a Chinese lantern and they had seen lots of them that night. I felt relieved and disappointed at the same time and thought that maybe we should all talk more to each other and everything would become clearer.

I got back into my car and started to head back west to my family with a new sense of hope. Maybe like Yuan-Xiao I had gone eastward to save myself from disappearing into a void from where I might never return. I decided that I couldn't leave behind a legacy where memories of me would be deformed by my temporary retreat into selfishness? My family no longer needed to see the miserable me and I decided that I needed to make more of an outward effort in order to ease their visible anguish. No higher power was about to apply a bit of make-up now, was he? From then on I would make more of an effort to appear content.

Talking about make-up Tam, do you know that in the more exclusive night clubs in the town they only let thin, good-looking people in? No kidding! It's all about appearance and they even employ people to constantly check their website to make sure there are no ugly minters in the promo pictures. I suppose, from a business point of view, it makes sense because the more people you pack in the more money that you are going to make. Some of the stewards on the doors are brutal and don't pull any punches and have no fear of offending anyone who doesn't fit the bill.

I knew this big guy whose nickname was Pharaoh and he worked on the door of a club down by the river and even if it was pouring with rain he got his kicks from making the 'fat and unsightly' wait about twenty minutes to find out if they were getting in or not. He was a beast and would fill the place to overflowing as long as it was packed with scrawny, anorexic looking chicks who might not spend very much on food but made up for it on drinks and entry money. The drinks in those sorts of places are always really expensive. So there was definitely no fat, skint people allowed. Who was it that said you can never be too thin or too rich? I can't remember.

Tam, I imagine you must know lots of heavy, unattractive people. You could help me set up a chain of clubs that are aimed at the fat, ugly, unemployed mob who could be given special discounts on Giro days. We could have security at the door with scales that would check that they were over a certain weight before gaining entry.

There must be a gap in the market for that eh Tam? We could invite big, fat celebrities to make special appearances. Oh my god, why has no-one thought of this before it's a fantastic idea.

Just think - a club where all the fatties could gorge themselves on food and drink, dressed in rags and revel within a gluttonous rabble who take no offence whatsoever when asked for an obesity identity card. They would need to have a BMI of at least thirty to get in and if it was any less than that then they would need to, at the very least, show signs of diabetes. We would want to attract the sort who would never think of drawing a knife in order to change the way they look for the sake of keeping others, who pass judgement on them, happy. Yes, I'm all for it and do you think it would be a good idea to give gingers a discount but they would still need to have a BMI of at least twenty-five? It would be dead easy to find a venue; some old warehouse with a concrete floor would be ideal.

"What do you view as a weakness?"

Tears are curious aren't they Tam and could be seen as a sign of weakness? They are the only things that come out of my body that I can recognise the taste of. I see no shame in licking them or just letting them drip onto a favourite shirt. You wouldn't really want to do that with any other excrement would you Tam? Well maybe you would but I would never, ever, for example, drink my own urine even if some people do see the health benefits of that. Tears are never really wasted though are they?

Do you know that there are three different types of tears? There are Basal ones that we need to keep our eyes from drying out. If we didn't have them, it would be really uncomfortable because our eyelids would need to scrape up and down against our eyeballs every time we blinked. Christ sake, could you imagine the discomfort; I mean life is hard enough without dry blinking.

My eyes are actually very sensitive and even the smallest things irritate them, which isn't helped by the fact that I love wearing mascara. That's the brown stuff that comes in a tube with a brush that goes on eyelashes Tam. You can get it in other colours but my preference is brown because of my ginger hair. Well, I know it's not that ginger now but old habits die hard you know. I think you would suit black with your colouring.

Where was I? Oh yes, onions, I absolutely hate peeling them and even the smallest little bugger has me irritated beyond belief. Even the reflex tears that are supposed to guard against this make little difference. Plus, I usually exacerbate the problem by wiping my face with an oniony hand and end up in a right old mess. I used to wonder if I used up all my tears and that one day there would be none left. What would that be like, I wonder, never to shed another tear? Ever! What if you think the worst thing has happened and then worse happens? There you are in a crowded room and get the worst news ever and everyone looks at you and expects you to burst into tears and you don't, and they're thinking, "Hard hearted bitch." but they don't know that they're all used up, you've none left. That would be a bastard that eh?

Your mob say that crying is therapeutic don't they? So what if there was that really, traumatic situation in my life and I lost the ability to cry because I'd peeled too many onions? Would I be in danger because I'd abused this important means of absolving physiological tension by preparing and eating a vegetable? Do you know that drinking onion juice mixed with honey is supposed to be good for the common cold? How ironic is it that? The fact that they make your eyes and nose run and then can also stop it makes it a very, crafty, little vegetable.

Men hate it when women start crying, don't they? I'm sure there's no better method of contraception than a woman starting to blubber. I suppose it's not any better if they burst out laughing either as that's a sure way to make your balls retract. I'd hate to have a penis and balls but men seem to be quite taken with them and very proud of their erections don't they? They wouldn't be quite so smart though if it was in the middle of their foreheads would they? Imagine cup final day and your team wins five nothing and there you all are, in the pub, all standing with your pints in hand, foreheads throbbing. No-one would need to wear colours would they? It would be quite evident who the winners were.

They also say that tears have hormones in them and I wonder if some men can sense that because my friend's brother used to always pick up women at funerals. He said that the scent of melancholy put him in the mood and he was always assured of sympathy shag when someone died. Do you think that women are actually addicted to sadness?

One of the things that definitely turn women off though is yon eau-de-poop, now that is a right turn-off and it has to be said that men shit and sweat a lot more than women. Put that along with the fact that we are more sensitive to smell and it's another no-brainer in the sex department. All that crap about animal magnetism doesn't wash with me at all. It's a wonder we're not extinct with the amount of stuff that puts us off having sex.

I know I said it before that I would never drink my own piss but I have put it to very good use in the past. You see I had this friend, well actually it was my husband but he would go mad if he thought I told anyone this. He had really smelly feet and we were working in Rimini, in August, so his problem was intensified by the heat. It was just awful and we had tried just about every potion available and then someone told him that steeping his feet in urine would help.

So there he was, every evening after work, peeing in the bidet and then sitting there with his feet in it, waiting for it to do its magic. However, he was really dehydrated because the temperature was hitting forty degrees and, although what he produced was of a very high intensity, there was never enough to cover his feet. The first time he asked me I gave an emphatic NO! Then I realised that it seemed to be making a difference so I gave in and donated my very own nectar and although it was weaker than his I produced much more, probably because I didn't sweat as much.

Eventually I did some research and found out that urine is not really waste, per se, but actually contains some nutrients such as minerals and proteins. This confused me Tam because we take time to eat good food and good care of ourselves and then, there we are, pissing it out again. So I suppose it might make sense to re-filter it by drinking or we could include it in risotto or something. I mean Salinger used to drink his own piss and he was a well-respected author; not mad at all so it's sort of acceptable I suppose. I might start writing! Then I could happily drink my piss all day long.

Also, they say tears shed laughing are the best medicine of all but I would much rather pee myself happy than shed miserable ones. Who? Well I don't know who. Check on that Wikipedia. Why the fuck you asking me that? I'm in the middle of telling you something important!

Ok, well.

What was I saying? Oh yes!

I'll never forget the day my husband came home from work and was absolutely raging because his friend told him that he had been taking the piss, about the smelly foot remedy and hoped he hadn't actually tried it. I actually had to lock myself in the bathroom and absolutely pissed myself laughing, can you believe that? They were taking the piss out of him, literally. But, the thing is, it worked but he wouldn't do it again so I was stuck with the stinking feet. Don't' know what was worse actually?

"Can you tell me about loss you have experienced?"

You know what Tam I'm always losing things? One of the first days I came here I lost my way and went into the wrong room. There was man sitting on the chair, right about where you are now, so I introduced myself and sat down. We sat there for what seemed like an eternity and then I noticed that he seemed to be looking for something in his pocket and he appeared a bit agitated. I thought he was looking for a pen but before I knew it he was all red in the face and was actually seeing himself off. I totally lost the plot and let him know, in no uncertain terms, what a dirty bastard he was.

The thing is because he was a bit scruffy and wearing cords I thought he was one of the doctors but it turned out that he was, in fact, another patient. He thought he'd hit the jackpot when I walked in. Seemingly, the day before, he suggested, because of the very close relationship with his mother, he would be able to expose more to a woman therapist. Well, I found that really interesting because of the fact that she appeared to be at the root of the problem. They had been sleeping in the same bed for most of his adult life. He took over when his dad buggered off with a man.

And how do I know this? Well, you lot need to be a bit more careful, because later that same day I found a notepad in the toilet with all the information on it. I know I shouldn't have read it but I couldn't help myself. It was really upsetting to be privy to such confidential information because the guy said that when I entered the room he felt aroused because I reminded him of his mother. Fuck sake, some of these people are mental.

After I lost my mother my sister brought me a set of worry beads from Greece. She also got some for herself and they are supposed to help you to lose weight; she was always starving herself trying to lose weight. She was stick thin already and all after I saw her all I did was worry about her. It's just as well they came with instructions or she might have bloody eaten them to ease her hunger pangs. Mine were amber coloured and the gentle clicking noise they made was supposed to help relax me and clear my mind. Not so. They caused me nothing but stress and the constant clicking nearly drove me mad.

I'd only had them for about a week when I 'mislaid' them. I spent hours wondering where they could be and retracing my steps to try to find them. Every time my sister phoned she would ask me if they were helping. I began to tell lies and make up stories about how relaxing they were and how people kept commenting on how beautiful they were. Maybe it was just as well I didn't find them because they say that amber represents a window to the past and *that* was what I was trying to forget. The thing is Tam I had put the beads in a safe place and couldn't remember where and I thought I was losing my mind. Fucking worry beads caused me nothing but stress.

You see my Grandpa had dementia and before he died he caused all sorts of mischief and mayhem. I say this because sometimes he would do things on purpose that he knew would really annoy my Gran then he'd catch my eye and give me a shifty wink. He never stopped doing that until the last time I saw him. My final memory of him was in the kitchen and he was helping to make the tea. We became aware of a strange smell and noticed smoke coming from the cooker where he'd placed the electric kettle to boil. While she was bawling and shouting at him he looked at me and there it was, that twinkle in his eye, just for me.

My Dad and my Grandpa were both called Patrick and every Saturday they would meet at the same bench down by the River Clyde near Hamilton. He always took my Dad a freshly, made sandwich because he hated the thought of him going for a drink on an empty stomach. Then, after he had eaten, they would take a stroll to the local pub and enjoy all the banter with the locals or go to watch the football. He was trying to keep my dad off the drink you see!

One Saturday though my Dad lost his watch and with it, all track of time. He got an earlier train than usual and decided to go into a pub near the station for a pint before getting to the usual rendezvous at the river. One drink led to another and by the time he went to look for Grandpa he had gone, so my Dad decided to make his way back to Glasgow, stopping at various hostelries on the way. When he eventually arrived at the house the police were there waiting for him. It was bad news.

All four of us were in the bedroom giggling and thinking how exciting it was and wondering what was going on. Listening behind the door we tried to hear what they were saying but the voices were muffled and nothing we heard made any sense. Suddenly we heard this roar that I will never forget. It reminded me of the wolfish cry that Heathcliff lets out when he's searching for Cathy and can't find her. You know, in that film. What's it called again.

My dear, sweet old grandpa had been found floating in the river and we never found out exactly what happened and how he ended up there. In the report it stated 'accidental death by drowning' and an autopsy revealed that he had eaten, probably a cheese sandwich, not long before he died. My dad lived 'til he was seventy-four and there was never a day in his 'puny being' that he didn't regret losing that watch. Robert Heap was spot on when he said that 'the knowledge of the correct time could be a matter of life or death'.

"Tell me about your aspirations."

If I could go back in time I would love to become an actress. Not the Hollywood type of star but a proper, tread the boards artist, who would live and breathe the job of bringing stories to life. I know it's a bit late to start now but I really do love being in a pretend space in my head, you know, somewhere calm and peaceful. It must be the best job in the world; to get up every day, dress up and speak like someone else, tell their story. I go to the theatre as much as I can and when I can't then I just travel to somewhere in my mind. My imagination has always been my saviour and the best way to escape the hassle and humdrum of all the shit that goes on in everyday life. Maybe someday someone, somewhere will play me in a film. How depressing would that be? Eh Tam?

"Where does your love of the theatre come from?"

Until I was about seven we lived in a tenement building in The Gorbals which was just round the corner from the Citizens Theatre and our flat was adjacent to the stage door. My sister and I used to stand down there at every chance we got and wait for the stars to arrive. Although we were in the middle of Glasgow, to us, it was like Hollywood. The actors were so glamorous and mysterious and it was the best thing in the world to be a part of, even in a small way. Some of them would stop and talk to us and we'd get them to sign our autograph books.

Then we'd go back up to the house and pretend to be them. Which is strange when you think about it because, there they were, down in the theatre, pretending to be other people and we were upstairs, pretending to be them. It makes me wonder if anyone really wants to be who they are. What do you think Tam? I bet you would like to be tall and handsome like a movie-star and get loads of attention from the ladies or the men, or maybe even both. Here I am telling you everything about me and I don't know anything about you do I?

"These sessions are for you to explore your own thoughts and ideas, not to learn more about me. Please continue."

Well, fine then, just trying to be friendly, but if you want to be like that, fine. What was I saying? Actors, my mum used to pretend to be an actual mother sometimes but the rest of the time she was trying to escape responsibility.

She used to try and emulate a character called Elsie Tanner, who was in Coronation Street and was played by an actress called Pat Phoenix, although my mum couldn't differentiate between the two. One evening my mother came with us to the stage door and nearly fainted when the actress stopped to speak to us. She kept calling her Elsie and said later that she sounded different in real life than she did on the telly and it must have been because of the part she was playing in the theatre.

My mother was quite a character on a Saturday night and when she got dressed up she used to talk in a different voice but instead of sounding like Elsie she sounded more like Dean Martin singing 'Lil' Old Wine Drinker'. When she tried to copy Elsie the preparations started first thing in the morning. She'd put in her curlers and refused to eat anything for the rest of the day because that made it easier to get her girdle up over her bumps. It also meant that she got drunk quicker but I'm sure that was not her intention.

I'll never forget that rubber contraption she called a roll-on. Why on earth it was called that I don't know because it took three of us about half an hour and a load of Johnston's baby powder to get it on. She would always leave it 'til the last minute because it was so uncomfortable and sometimes when she got home drunk it would be in her bag. I even remember being mortified when I was sent along to the pub the next day to ask if she had left it in the toilet. We had such a laugh about it especially when I pretended to personify the girdle and recount a story from the night before. We even gave it a name, Gertrude Tricky Fatulandoff. Or GTF for short!

Like Elsie Tanner, my mum had gorgeous, red hair and shared the same kind of temperament. She was always sad and lonely and suffered because of her bad choice in men. They both also bore terrible losses; in my mother's case it was three children she lost. One was only six weeks old, another six months and the eldest was twenty-nine. The babies died of 'cot deaths' and the priest said it was 'God's will' and she needed to get over it, move on with her life and rely on her faith to lead her through the darkness. He said this while drinking a glass of whisky and smoking a cigarette. Everyone seemed to smoke in those days and that, along with the fire churning out stinking fumes, was enough to make anyone bloody choke, never mind a new born baby.

Another thing I remember is the incredible stench of those fire-lighter things and this one time my brother had to be rushed to hospital because he tried to eat one of them. They were kept in the cupboard under the sink along with the black, stinking disinfectant and the bleach. He was always crawling in there searching for things to eat and play with. My mother was also partial to that black cleaning fluid and I remember seeing her one day with a cloth over her mouth, sniffing it, and her face was stained. Years later when I asked her about that she said that had been a notion she had because of the pregnancy.

Elsie Tanner was once described by the Prime Minister as "the sexiest thing on television". I suppose my Mum was trying to be sexy in her own way. She would go out looking fabulous and smelling like a baby and when she got back she stank like a brewery and looked like a tramp. I hated to see her like that. Then she would sing melancholy songs, cry and tell us how much she missed my Dad. I would kiss her face and wipe the tears away but it was never enough. Nothing seemed to make any difference about the way she felt. It's funny, isn't it, that people can have family around them that would do anything for them; steal, lie, even change their own path in life, but all they long for is something or someone else. She always longed for something else. Do you think you can die of longing Tam? Is that an actual thing? What would you put on the death certificate? Cause of death: Yearning!

When my mum died it was my job to get her clothes ready. I bought most of them for her you see. She hated going shopping for clothes and was a 'bit on the heavy side'. She nearly always wore black and just loved dressing things up with jewellery and scarves. It was an easy job for me because I knew exactly what made her feel good. I even wondered if I should put some perfume in but felt a bit silly asking the people at the Co-Op too many questions so I sprayed it on the clothes before putting them in the bag.

On the night before the funeral I had a dream that she came into my room and sat on the edge of the bed. She asked me what she would be wearing. I explained that I had picked a chiffon blouse with wide sleeves because I knew she was so self-conscious about her arms. A black skirt with an elasticated waist which was ideal as I didn't want her to feel uncomfortable. She then asked me what jewellery she would be wearing and I let her into a secret and told her that my husband had bought her beautiful, crystal earrings as a table gift for Christmas day. She said that would be lovely as it was very dark where she was and they would add sparkle; make her feel a bit brighter and more glamorous.

On the day of the funeral I got back to the house and was sitting staring at her picture on the sideboard when suddenly the sun shone in the window and hit something which sent sparkles all around the room. It was the earrings. I'd forgotten to put them in the bag that I'd taken to the undertakers. From that day till this, they just sit there, on the same spot and I long for a moment, when the room comes alive with the sparkle and I'm touched by her presence. I always keep baby powder in the house and although it is very drying on the skin I sometimes shake it into my bathrobe. I've never told anyone this before Tam but every now and again I even sniff a fire-lighter - it just depends in the mood I'm in.

When I have a bit more time I might do an acting course, nothing too intense, just for fun. I mean what could be better than becoming someone else for a few hours and being able to say things that you would never say yourself. Actually I've heard that the NHS Trust have proposed a stand-up comedy course for people with mental health problems. That is such a great idea isn't? That would be really interesting, people with depression, getting out of bed, standing up, telling jokes. Why did no-one think of it sooner? I'm sure the BBC would throw money at it! What do you think they would call it Tam, 'Stand and Recover' or 'Convalescent Comedy? You're not very funny are you Tam? Can't imagine you ever making anyone laugh, ever.

"Do you have any siblings?"

One sister and three brothers.

Are you deliberately trying to upset me? I fucking told you about the babies that died. Fucking torture this. You're supposed to be trying to help me. How is this helping? Maybe you should write all this down and stop ticking, fucking boxes.

I had four brothers but three of them died. Ok, four minus three equals one. I have one brother left but might never see him again if you keep forgetting things and I have to keep repeating myself. Fuck sake. I'll end up like Alan Cummings in *Macbeth*, repeating the script, playing all the characters, every day. He was in a lunatic asylum too you know. The character in the play, not Alan Cummings. What about Macbeth? He went mental didn't he? Or was it his wife? I'm getting all mixed up today. What did you ask me? Oh yes, siblings!

It was 1992 and the beginning of the end of my relationship with my mother. My youngest brother, was great, always smiling, in fact, I worked with a girl and her dad used to be a warden in Barlinnie prison and she told me that they called him 'smiler'. Seemingly the staff thought he was really funny. So that was nice, that the warden liked him, and remembered him, in a good way. It gave me some comfort knowing somebody, somewhere, other than us, remembered him.

I remember one of the times my mum 'took to her bed' I heard a noise in the room, and there he was, standing over her, in the dark and I shouted at him because I thought he was trying to find her bag and maybe steal some money. What he *had* been doing was putting a hot water bottle under the covers, at her feet, in case she was cold. I said I was sorry but he ran out and slammed the door. The next time I saw him he was in intensive care and my mother was sitting beside *his* bed. I felt as if it was my fault he was there. If only I hadn't shouted at him. If only, I hadn't gone into the room. If only he hadn't started taking drugs. If only?

He was in the first bed when you entered the ward. The lights were dim and the bed was tilted upwards. I thought it was strange that his head was lower than his feet but I didn't think to ask why. Isn't that strange that they positioned him in that way? He looked so uncomfortable, it really upset me. I wanted to hold his head up and let him know I was there and let him how much I loved him. He had been beaten up by a group of guys; all of them were from the same family. I think they were called Donnelly or Connelly, I don't really remember? They were from a well-known Irish, Catholic family.

It had happened late on the Saturday night. He'd met a young man he knew and he was in an awful state. Someone had taken him to a party and when he got there a man had taken him into a room and molested him. My brother took him to our house and assured him that he would take care of things and no one else needed to know what had happened. The next time my brother saw the older, queer guy he just went for him and gave him a right beating. He had only been defending his wee pal you see and it turned out to be a big mistake. The molester and his four brothers came after *him,* my brother and that's why he ended up there, in that bed, critical. Battered senseless.

The next twenty-four hours were crucial they said. My Mother was hysterical, saying it was all her fault, if she had not been drinking, if she had taken better care of us, if this, if that. What the fuck was she talking about? It would not have made a blind bit of difference. He was there because he was a good guy and he cared about what happened to people. He was simply looking after his friend. Suddenly it was all about her, everyone was trying to calm her, saying "It's all right, you'll be fine, don't worry, he'll pull through." "You've done your best." Did she fuck. She was useless. A disgrace of a woman.

He did pull through though and made a full recovery. Well sort of, he wasn't dead, not yet. They had given him so many drugs that when he got out of hospital the prescriptions were never enough. He began to ache for erstwhile solutions to ease the pain. Just this once, just for today; he told us he could stop when he wanted. They all think that. If only he had faced reality and been able to fight his demons. I begged him to get help and he went to see the doctor and was given Temazepam! Fucking Temazepam, can you believe it?

There was no coming back from that hell because it was totally acceptable to take something that was prescribed by the doctor. No stigma with that. They know best after all, don't they Tam? They are the professionals with whom we entrust our lives. What other options do we have? Buying drugs from dealers is dangerous after all. The trouble is that on the day my brother died he had visited both experts and there are no co-ordinators between the legal agents and the scum on the street.

"How was he after that?"

Although it was inevitable. It's still such a shock when it happens. My husband and children had gone to Italy for a month and I couldn't go with them because of my work commitments. I was missing them dreadfully and managed to get a week off and booked a last minute ticket. The flight was from Manchester and my Dad lived there so it meant I could visit him at the same time. I was so excited that I thought my head was going to explode.

Dad met me from the train and we went out for dinner and had a couple of drinks. We were sitting chatting when the phone rang. It was my mother and she was hysterical. She had gone to stay at my sister's in London and nothing either of them said to me made any sense. 'He's dead', they repeated over and over. I hung up on them and tried to contact someone in Glasgow but my hands were shaking so much and my mind was racing so it was very difficult and reluctantly I dialled 999.

Do you know that when you contact the emergency services they put you through to the relevant department and then they stay on the phone to make sure you are all right? Isn't that really thoughtful? Each time I spoke to someone the girl I contacted initially was still there, on the line, asking if I was okay and who I needed to speak to next. I told her that my flight was leaving in a couple of hours and that I was going to surprise my family and she suggested that maybe I should let them know what had happened and cancel the flight.

When I eventually decided to get on the flight to Italy I was in a right state and all of the airline staff were very kind and tried to soothe me but I just kept repeating that he was dead and telling them how much

I loved him. As soon as the flight took off I knew I'd made a mistake and should have gone home to Glasgow. He was on his own, in the mortuary, cold, on a slab. They sat me away from the other passengers and when we got to the airport they let me off first and escorted me through customs to where my husband and his friend were waiting. The thing I wanted most in the world was to see my two lovely children and take them in my arms and kiss them 'til my lips hurt as much as my heart.

It was the Glasgow Fair holiday and all the airlines were really busy and I couldn't get a flight back and had to come back on my original ticket. Even if I had managed to buy another seat my insurance would not have covered the cost as it was a 'drugs related death'. It didn't matter one iota that the only drug *I* took were painkillers and that it was me who actually paid for the insurance in the first place. No way would they pay out. That's the law according to corporate profiteering.

My mother never did forgive me and could not believe that I still 'went on holiday' even though her son had died. She was never the same after that. Not with me, or anyone for that matter. Her most important relationship became the one she had with a bottle. It was so sad but at times she would come back to us and be her fabulous, funny self that everyone loved to be with. Then she would remember and would leave us again. All I could do was wait and savour the scraps of love and discernment that were handed out to me by this woman whom I adored to my very core.

"What was your education like?"

I loved everything about being in school, from the stodgy food to the scratchy toilet paper. I flitted between schools sixteen different times and lived in, approximately, thirty-two homes in my formative years. So I'm quite the expert in the fields of both education and home removals. Maybe someday I'll write a book about it and call it 'The Value of a Veritable and Varied Education'. It would celebrate the virtues of an unstable childhood and promote the skills that can be garnered from orphaned children living with remote parents.

We were always flitting about and being evicted so I'm very adept at packing a suitcase, or a box, in a hurry. Once, we even packed up the whole house when my Dad was at work. The only transport my Mum could afford was the scrap-man's horse and cart. So, there we were, going from The Gorbals to Bridgeton through the Glasgow Green like a scene from the *OK Corral*. I was euphoric and pretended to be Scarlet O'Hara being taken in a carriage to my new home in the East End. That was a lovely day, although it was more 'taking the piss' than '*Gone with the Wind*' and all the neighbours laughed their heads off at us. I didn't care though because for a day I had been someone who didn't give a damn what anyone thought. I was a rebel and would worry about what they thought tomorrow. After all, tomorrow is another day.

By the time I was fifteen and we had, yet another, house move I resolutely refused to move school because I only had a year to go before I finished school for good. The authorities classed me as a fee paying pupil because I lived out with the catchment area and I had to pay my own bus fare. My God, I thought that was marvellous and very posh at the time. I had been 'classed' for the first time! I was a different class from everyone else and this time my carriage was a corporation bus instead of a horse drawn carriage.

The staff at the schools must have had a right, old guffaw when we enrolled, at the same school, for the fourth time:

> "Here they come again, the jelly-shoed vagabonds."
> "Charge of the ginger brigade."
> "Wonder how long they will last this time?"

Even my granny used to talk about us and say:

> "Those poor weans down in Glasgow having to
> go to school wearing those plastic shoes."

Later in life, when I thought about her, in her big house with more than enough money, I could never understand why she didn't just buy us some fucking shoes. If she had been that concerned, or ashamed, that's all she had to do, cough up a few quid. I hated her so much. I called her 'The Old Reptile'. We had to knock her living room door and she would shout, "Enter" as though she was the bloody queen. An old lounge lizard, that's what she really was. I'm called after her you know? Well you didn't, but you do now. Oh, I told you that already, did I? Sorry, I'm repeating myself. I might change my name to something like…? Not sure would need to think about that for a while.

I remember getting these really beautiful shoes and wore them 'til the soles fell off. These men had come to the door selling them. They were Italian and my mum bought a pair for me and my sister but they were not the right sizes. I'm talking about the shoes not the men who were selling them by the way. My sister's shoes were two sizes too big and she was a size six anyway and mine were too small. I ended up being off school for ages. My feet became really infected because even although I had developed big, pussy blisters I still insisted on wearing them. What started as a dream became a shoe nightmare. Nothing ever went quite as I fancied.

Even in my imagination I could never be Cinderella in those shoes. I still loved them though and used to keep them under my pillow in case they got nicked. I had this friend and she was so funny and I remember once we were on a school trip and I had fallen asleep with my feet up and everyone could see the cardboard through the hole in the sole of my shoe. She made everyone laugh by shouting:

"Any money for the Holy Souls?"

It was hilarious. Everyone was pissing themselves laughing. Yes, she was a good friend, really funny. People laughed a lot when we were about. We didn't have to do much to raise a giggle.

God, that's reminded me of another school trip that came up and it was also a bit of a nightmare because I was staying in a Salvation Army hostel with my Mum at the time. No-one at the school knew where I was staying as I didn't expect to be there for too long. It was in a beautiful building on Clyde Street near the city centre and believe it or not, it is now classed as a Historical Monument by the Royal Commission, imagine that? I was becoming right posh, first staying with the Queen of Hamilton, paying my fees in order to get to school and then, there I was, living in a Monument. No wonder I began to think I was a princess or a film star and that someone had made a mistake and sent me to the wrong address; about thirty different times.

When we stayed there I had to get up at six o'clock each morning in order to take a bus journey past the school and then get another one from the opposite direction so that I could pretend to be living at my aunt's house. She had a lovely, big house just outside of Glasgow with gardens at the front and back. It was fabulous being able to say that I was living at her house, even though I wasn't. Anyway I soon got found out.

We were going to the Herald offices to see the newspaper going out to print. First I had to get permission from the Sergeant at the hostel in order to get my late pass because the doors were locked at ten. Seriously, it was as if I'd signed up for the foreign legion. Then, I had to let the Modern Studies teacher know because I'd need to be last off the bus, so that none of the other pupils would find out where I was staying. The teacher was very kind and her face was all soft and sympathetic. She told me not to worry that it would be our secret. The fuck it was!

The next day was like a horrible dream with big, pathetic marshmallowy faces coming at me from all angles:

> *"Hi, are you OK? Is everything alright?"*
> *"You look lovely today?"*

"How is your Mum?"

"How are you today? If you need anything just ask."

What? Were they going to club together and buy us a house and get my brothers out of the children's home? Some of these teachers had never even acknowledged me before and there they were, concerned and sympathetic. So much for confidential information being shared on a 'need to know' basis! I ended up arriving at classes late and sitting in the toilet at break time so that I didn't need to speak to anyone. I couldn't keep up with the lies I was telling and hated the attention I was getting for living such an extraordinary life. My imagination could not keep up with the reality.

Every bugger who worked in the school knew where I was staying. So I decided then and there not to tell anyone anything about me ever again. I was fed up being laughed at and people offering false hope and sympathy when they didn't really care. I decided to make up stories and my life became much more colourful and instead of feeling sorry for me they were genuinely interested in what I had to say. I wasn't really telling lies or anything, just not telling the truth, the whole truth and nothing but the truth, so help me Tam!

I stayed on for an extra year and was one of the first pupils ever to do that at our school. Most of the others could not get out fast enough but I felt a sense of security and order when I was there and never wanted to leave. Years after I left I would dream of being in school and walking through the corridors floating in and out of each room. Sometimes I would know I was dreaming and try to make it last longer by not opening my eyes and just imagining I was there. Strange that isn't? It was always that same school, where the teachers had shown the insincere concern.

In those days we got paid for staying on at school, it was called a bursary but I was too young to get it in my name so it was signed over to my Mother. There were parties every night for at least a week, thanks to me being so clever and all. She, my mother eventually made a contribution to my 'education' by buying me a hair-dryer which could not be used because most of the time the electricity was turned off. She thought that if my hair was nicer then I would be more confident and would 'take more in'. Clean, dry hair was the way forward in education. She was inspiring, my Mum.

Later that year my friend and I were selected to go to a big, posh conference at Jordanhill, which was the teacher training college. We felt dead important to be asked and it was the first time that anyone from our school had ever attended. All the other kids had school uniforms on so we made up a big story about forgetting it was a school day and pretending we thought it was like a day off and that's why we were not wearing ours. Our school didn't have a uniform policy as they would have been farting against thunder trying to get us to wear them anyway.

There was a question and answer session at the end of the conference and my friend and I asked the most interesting ones and everyone clapped and looked at us in amazement. We didn't actually understand what the question was because our teachers had written them for us to take with us. Everyone thought we were dead clever, considering 'where we came from'. We had just been to the toilet and so we decided there was nothing to this intelligence carry-on and most of these people were not quite right. How could going to the lavvy make you ask better questions?

Also, there was a coffee break, imagine that, a coffee break, for school children, we had finally arrived. We said we didn't like coffee and they had to go and get us a pot of tea and we were dead chuffed because we had people running after us. However back at the school when we told the English teacher about this he was so disappointed and told us that coffee was an acquired taste. If we wanted to get on in life, we really had to learn to enjoy it.

What a revelation that was, to get on, all we had to do was like coffee. I was so inspired that I decided, then and there, that I would become a teacher and change people's lives with my wisdom. My vocation was to spread the word about Cappuccino, Latte, Espresso and the like. For the next two weeks we made ourselves sick ordering coffee in the local cafe and forcing ourselves to drink it. The results were truly astonishing. I have never had so much energy in my whole life. It was fantastic.

We started to run everywhere and became very enthusiastic about everything. My pal's sister worked in the cafe and we got it for free but when I asked my Mum to buy some I got all the usual comments like, "Who the fuck do you think you are, staying on at school, reading fucking books all the time, drinking bloody coffee?" That sort of took away the joy of our new discovery and the excitement of our beautiful and inspiring proclamations about education.

Anyway, I had to leave school soon after that and pinned all my hopes and dreams on exotic drinks and self-help books. One of the best books I ever read taught me that one should always leave some food on 'one's plate' and know the value of owning at least three bras; one black and two skin coloured. That was a very educational book. Life changing actually.

If I remember the name of it, I'll let you know Tam. Not that I think you are in need of any grooming tips or anything. I'm sure that, in this kind of job, it's important for you to be comfortable and not be too concerned about what you look like.

"How long does it take you to fall asleep?"

Well, to tell you the truth, the times vary. Some nights I just pass out but that's usually after a couple of glasses of good red and other times I can be awake all night. One night that was particularly bad – actually it turned out to be a great adventure. I was very agitated and began to feel really hungry, so I got up and went to the kitchen. I really wanted some chocolate and there was nothing of that ilk in the house, so I decided to go for a walk to the local garage.

On the way there I could not stop thinking about the brown stuff, but Mars Bars in particular. The craving got so bad that I started to run and got so fast that I thought I was flying. Eventually I got there and, can you believe this, they didn't have any? What all night petrol stations don't have any fucking Mars Bars? I mean it is only one of the top selling products in the world and it is a delicacy here in Scotland with about 20% of chip shops selling them deep fried!

Anyway, I then decided to go on to the local chip shop. Well actually, by this point, nothing was really local as I had gone quite far, about two miles away. That's how determined I was to fulfil this craving, and what do you know? None! Can you honestly believe that?

By this point I was in a rage and beginning to feel like Michael Douglas in that film 'Falling Down'. I then remembered that there was an all-night supermarket near the house. I had forgotten they had started to open all night. So off I trailed, got there and lo and behold, there they were, on the counter, all black and red wrapped. I was on another planet.

Shoving it in my pocket I headed back to the house and when I arrived

I went straight into bed. Then, you'd never credit it, just as I was unwrapping it I let it drop under the duvet. So, there I was, under the covers looking for the bloody thing when my husband hit me on the head and asked me what I was doing? I told him I was looking for my Mars Bar.

He gave me such a look and told me, then and there, that I really needed to see a doctor, as soon as possible. You see, there was no Mars Bar! He did say however that he was glad that I had not actually found it and taken a bite as that might have landed us in A & E.

Imagine having to explain that to a doctor. I would have been certified for sure:

> *"Hallo, would Mrs Section 24 please come to cubicle number 13 please!"*

We were both really tired that week as my nocturnal escapades were becoming a regular occurrence. Just a few nights before the episode with the chocolate he had woken up to find me on the exercise bike, stark naked, pedalling away. We were both really tired the day after that I can tell you.

"Do you experience any feelings of anxiety?"

Sometimes I get so anxious going to bed that my heart races and it makes me feel sick. Do you ever get that? It's horrible. Then if I do get to sleep I wake up and start calculating how much time there is left. Looking at the clock and wishing there was someone to talk to and feeling so alone.

I used to get up and watch telly and maybe open a bottle of wine but that really got me into trouble because one morning I forgot about that and went to work in the car. That ended really badly - but I don't want to talk about that. Well not now anyway...

I always find it hard to sleep when I go on holiday or when I stay at someone else's house. It's a wonder I slept at all when I was small as we were always flitting about, sleeping in different places; strangers' houses. I remember one of the times we went on our travels. Big journey. Bridgeton to Easterhouse, only about four miles but it seemed further at the time. Public transport you see.

My Mum put all of our stuff in the big pram she used for the laundry, sometimes she even used it for the baby, and off we went on this epic journey to Easterhouse. We were heading to the house of a friend of hers. It was a new house in one of the schemes. It had three bedrooms and a fitted kitchen, 'all the mod cons' my Mother said. It would be great. Like a wee holiday.

When we eventually got there; no one was in so my mother decided to break in. She smashed the bathroom window and lifted my brother carefully through to go and open the door. She said the lady wouldn't mind at all, she was a good pal. Not sure that the council, who actually owned the property, would have been so enamoured. She would be too pleased to see us to bother about a broken window. And so she was, really pleased especially with the pram full of booze my mother brought! She even threw a party in our honour. Invited all the degenerates in the neighbourhood. Everywhere we went it was like party central.

That particular night my sister and I were really tired and when all the adults were in full drinking mode we went into one of the rooms and onto a big double bed. It was a great, big, soft and comfy bed I quickly drifted off. Later, I don't know how long it was, I woke up, two people came into the room. 'Til this day I don't know who they were but I knew I had to keep very still and not say a word. They were whispering and as they entered the room I could already smell the drink and mixed with the stench of tobacco.

They propped themselves on the bottom edge of the bed and were talking in very low voices at first and then they started to make funny, animal-like noises and the bed was squeaking as they bounced up and down. I pulled my feet up very quickly and I nearly giggled...but I didn't. I didn't want to get into any trouble because I'm not sure if we were supposed to be in the bed in the first place. I was afraid if they knew I was awake they might want me to join in the game. I wondered if my sister was awake, but I never did ask her and 'til this, day I've never spoken about it. It was years before I realised what those people had been doing. I was only about seven at the time and, to me, it sounded like fun, as if they were bouncing and bobbing up and down.

When my girls were young, and we had company in our house, I was always very aware of where people were. If anyone had gone anywhere near my girls, I would have known. Absolutely! It was, and still is, my job to look after them and make sure they come to no harm. Children are so precious and vulnerable; they need to be protected don't you think, Tam?

My Mother had simply been too busy enjoying the party to know what was going on in that room. It's not as if she had forgotten about us or anything. She just stopped thinking about us for a while because she was having such a good time. I'm sure that it wasn't her in the room with the other person, the man. I'm absolutely positive of that. I would have known. I'm sure I would have known if it had been her...

"What's your mood first thing in the morning?"

God knows, sometimes I'm scared to open my eyes. I remember one, beautiful morning I woke up really early and heard the doorbell. I floated downstairs and, looking through the glass door, could see my brother and a friend. It was really great to see him as it had been a long time, a very long time since I last saw him. Anyway, they came in and went into the living room and I went into the kitchen to make some tea.

It turned out that John's mother worked beside me but he could not remember what department. We laughed so much and they told me great stories about things they had done together when they were younger. They were always up to something those two.

Once, years before, they'd gone to my mother's house in The Gorbals with a beautiful and very ornate mirror and asked her to keep it for them "'til later" as they had to deliver it to someone who wasn't home from work yet. She said that would be fine and asked them where they had got it from and they said it had fallen from the back of a lorry. Back of a lorry, a mirror and she believed them!

My Mum was so naive and they were so plausible that she accepted this explanation and said to me that it was amazing that the mirror hadn't broken in the fall. You know what I think Tam? I think she did know what they were up to and her naivety was simply a coping mechanism in order to defend him when she needed to.

After they left my house that morning I went back to bed and fell sound asleep until my alarm went off at seven. It felt really nice when I thought about what had happened in my encounter with my funny, lovable rogue of a brother and as I crept down the stairs I had a dreadful sense of apprehension and elation at the same time.

There were no dirty cups, no biscuit wrappers, no squashed cushions, cigarette butts, no scent of him. That wonderful…. cold, damp, musty, fearful, desolate, desperate and despondent smell he had when he used to arrive at my house, in the middle of the night, when he had nowhere else left to run was gone. Then I remembered he was dead.

Feeling really down I went into work and one of my colleagues asked me what was wrong and I told her about my dream and how good I'd felt when I woke up. We got to talking about dreams and what they could mean and I told her that John had given me a message to give to his mum and that I was to tell her that he was OK and hoped that she had enjoyed reading his journal.

At this she went as white as a sheet and told me that Marie who worked in the canteen had a son called John, he had died in a car accident and she took great comfort in reading his diary. She found it underneath his pillow after he died. He had started writing it during a school trip and had written how much he missed her and that he couldn't wait to come home.

You know something Tam, I hate waking up too early? Especially if I'm having a nice dream. I try to go back into the dream and I can't. It's okay if you have another few hours to sleep but if it is just about time to get up it really messes up the rest of the day and makes you feel down and very tired, exhausted. Doesn't it? Do you ever get that? Are you okay Tam? You seem a bit tired. Should we have a wee break? I'm tired today; extremely tired so maybe we should take a break.

"Do you often feel sad?"

Do you mean am I feeling sad now, because I'm not but it might not take much to bring it on so you better be careful what you ask me today Tam? In fact, this morning I woke up laughing. I had a dream that I was a duck and took my period and every time I tried to insert a tampon I fell over. It was so funny. There I was, quacking away hysterically and struggling with a soggy plug. Yes, I was in a pond while this was going on. What a great way to start the day eh?

Do you know what makes me really angry though? Sometimes you can just be going about your business and enjoying the day and something happens to upset you. Like you're not even the least bit melancholy and wham, someone or something bursts your bubble and your flimsy spirit is too weak to deny access and it all comes flooding right in. For instance, going to get a new passport should be an exciting thing to do but can, all of a sudden, turn into a life changing drama.

It's all arranged, the holiday is booked, the clothes have been bought, feet have been sorted out, your fat china has been groomed to perfection, which is a must because mine are not very attractive and need all the help they can get. Actually I meant my feet are attractive because I obviously only have the one vagina. Have you seen those fish pedicures? I've had it done twice and it is fabulous. Don't know if I would go too late in the day though because I'm not sure how hungry they would be so I would always go first thing in the morning when they're really starving and they'd eat away all the badness in my feet. Imagine asking one of them what they had for breakfast.
"Oh just a couple of corns with a wee topping of verruca."
Sounds quite appetizing actually. You would probably agree that

I'm at my best this morning, eh Tam? I'm feeling great this morning and looking forward to everything. Even chatting to you.

Anyway, back to the holiday and just when I thought everything was done, I noticed that my passport was out of date with less than a week 'til take off. After the initial, panicky call to the office I realised that it could be sorted, at a cost. One hundred and eighty pounds to be exact but in the scheme of things, it's fine besides, the trip couldn't go ahead without one. Seemingly, in the old days you could leave the country without one but you wouldn't get back in again.

So, be prepared because this is what happens Tam, off you go with the old document and, on the way to the passport office, you stop at the photo booth in Asda. Then bam! There you are; ten years older but not feeling any wiser, staring back at yourself. Hello, this is what you really look like. Head spinning, you go and sit down to get over the shock and try to figure out what happened to the other you, the one that had to be renewed and you start to think about the time in between and then, if you're unlucky, all the memories come flooding back.

Neither my mum nor my dad ever had a passport, isn't that sad? I'd like to say it didn't matter and they were quite happy as they were but I'd be lying. They were miserable most of the time but maybe it would have been different if they'd travelled, seen other parts of the world and experienced different cultures. They might have shed their inherited traits and found a way of nurturing their best qualities towards creating a life that would embrace all six of us.

Instead of staying up all night drinking and fighting they could have read us stories 'til the words drifted away just as sunbeams lit up the room and birdsong lulled us to sleep all day, instead of going to school. Then, in the afternoon, I could have read *my dad* adventure stories while he cleaned his *own* shoes as my mum prepared a lunch of chocolate cake, eve's pudding and strawberry milkshakes. Instead they were absent in their neglect and my sister, brothers and I struggled to be everything to each other in spite of this hopeless pair. We were fucking orphans living in the same house as out parents.

We all struggled through though and for the most part all did quite well for ourselves and over the years things take a turn anyway, don't they? Children eventually become the carers and parents need to be looked after. It's at these times we have to overlook the past and move on in order to live with each other and find some common ground.

Filling in forms was always a problem for both of them and don't even get me started on those automated answering machines. My mother once tried to order a new wheelie bin and nearly ended up adopting three Somalian children. I knew she had done something wrong when she said that one of the questions they asked was if she had recently undergone fertility treatment. She thought it was something to do with recycling compost and decided to keep all her used teabags in anticipation.

My dad was so hopeless with anything technical and it was dead funny. I remember trying to explain to him how mobile phones worked. The first time he ever saw one was when I went to see him in Manchester. Not many people had them at the time and it was a bit of a novelty. We had gone out for a meal to Coco's, which was my favourite place, and while we were there my husband phoned me. Afterwards, my Dad looked puzzled and asked me how he had known where we were. At first I did not know what he meant and then when I realised I thought I was going to have a heart attack laughing.

Two days later I was still trying to explain to him how they worked. I explained time and time again that people phoned the phone and not a specific location but he was not convinced. The concept was totally lost on him. He was very suspicious of them and would move away when I was talking to anyone in case he got traced by the social security. He did eventually get one but only ever used it to phone me and in between times took the battery out so that he couldn't be traced and have his money stopped.

Right up until the day he died he kept saying that he was hoping to sit his driving test and go to see his brother in Brighton. I'm sure he didn't really want to go or he would have just got the bus or the train. Even in his hospital bed, when he knew he was dying, he spoke about driving down to see Johnny. That's not his real name you know but, he's still there and still alive, so I need to keep it a bit of a secret, just in case! He lived there for years, hiding from something. I used to think they were making it all up but then I realised that is was something quite serious that kept him away.

This brother is a bit of an enigma. We can only contact him through a P.O. Box number that only two people know. They never trusted my dad with anything as he would have blurted it out to everyone when he'd had a beverage. Very strange it was. I once asked a policeman friend of mine what he thought of it and he said that it was probably something to do with a murder or maybe a robbery.

Sometimes he would turn up at funerals and leaves very quickly afterwards. My uncle that is, not the policeman.

When we were small I loved him so much and he used to tell us great stories but if someone came to the door he'd disappear up to the loft and we would not see him again for ages. My Dad looked up to him and gave him total respect even though he was his younger brother. I think he would've liked to have lived that sort of life, ducking and diving, living a bit like a gangster. Doing what he wanted all the time with no responsibility except to himself. Actually…that sort of describes him anyway!

My dad loved the 'Rat pack' and would watch all the old Frank Sinatra stuff and documentaries about boxing and he absolutely loved Mohammed Ali, who was his hero. He did some boxing in his younger days and always wanted to train young boys to fight but never really got around to it. He adored 'The Untouchables' on a Saturday night and used to go on about the characters as if they were real, as if he knew them.

He lived in a fantasy world and it was all rather sad if you think about it. I used to imagine what it was like for him when he was away, living in another city. I thought about him telling people about his wife and children and how much he wanted to be with them and live happily ever after. Now that would have been a great story. I'd like to find out more about my uncle though, that would be an interesting tale to tell the grand kids wouldn't it? Instead of spurting all this shite to you

Well, this has been quite nice this morning Tam, thinking about the past and not really feeling sad or dredging up old muck has been very refreshing. It's nice to know that sometimes I can reflect on my past and know that some of it was quite positive and a lot of it was actually tinged with happiness. I can tell by the look on your face that you found all of this exhilarating Tam. Tam, Tam, times up…wakey wakey!

"Have you experienced a decrease in appetite?"

Only when I'm in love, or sad, or worried or trying to lose weight but not that often really. My first love? Well actually Tam, I can quite clearly see now it wasn't love at all, it was more of a misunderstanding. It was a time when was when I was at my thinnest, a size six/eight, fabulous. Although at that time a size six didn't exist, it seems to be a new thing. We would have said too skinny instead of six. My friends were so jealous and said it was 'just the ticket' what they needed, a bastard of a man, an urban hooligan, just for a while, a bit of heartbreak and maybe a wee skelp on the mouth. Then they could shift some weight. Our idea of the dream guy was the one that helps you lose a few pounds; destroys everything about you and leaves you so distraught that you even lose the capacity to grieve. Prince fucking charming!

At first I steered well clear of him because I knew that his type were all the same, flashing the cash and bragging about how they 'earned' it and deluding themselves into thinking they were modern day Robin Hoods. Although I knew it was wrong, I still found him interesting and he made me laugh so much by telling me funny stories about robbing banks, jumping payrolls and how he was on the verge of a really big job that would let him thousands. I told him that I would help him to write a book and we would call it 'Tales of Robbing Hoodlums' or, as it should have been, a 'Guide to Being a Total Prick'.

He told me his sister had managed to get a job in a posh clothes shop in town and knew all the details of when the payroll was delivered and the system used for takings cash to the bank. At that time wages were given out in pay packets and not paid into accounts the way they are now. The plan was to strike at the Glasgow, Fair holiday when the payroll would be double and the takings high. He explained that two of the staff would be responsible for taking the black bags containing the money and cheques along the main street to deposit them into the night safe. His sister was on the rota for that shift and would leave a window open to allow them into the shop to take the pay packets from the safe, for which they had the combination. Dead easy! I listened and laughed but thought he was having one of his Walter Mitty moment.

I had arranged to go and visit friends in Edinburgh and when I got back on the Sunday night my mum was waiting for me and brought my attention to a headline in the newspaper. It stated that some poor bloke had been beaten to a pulp and was in critical after a robbery in the town on the Saturday night. I knew by the look on her face that she thought it had something to do with him because I had told her the story. At the time we'd laughed so hard that the tears streamed down our cheeks but no one was laughing now and I felt sick to my stomach.

One of his pals came round to my house to tell me he'd fled to Spain for a while. He said 'not to worry' and to make sure that, if anyone, especially the police, asked, I was to say that I'd been away for the weekend and knew nothing. That's exactly why he'd encouraged me to go and had even given me spending money, because he didn't want me implicated in any way. Wasn't that thoughtful Tam? I said I didn't care if I never saw him again and decided then and there that anything we had was over. It had been fun for a while but I hardly knew him. All I could think about was that poor young man lying in the hospital and how his family must have been feeling. The thought of him coming near me or ever touching me, ever again, made my skin crawl and I couldn't believe that I had been taken in by such a mean bastard. Then, a couple of weeks later, he turned up!

I was babysitting for a friend of my mum's in the flats across the road. The children were asleep and there was a knock at the door. The couple weren't expected back until ten thirty and it was only half past eight. I looked through the keyhole and there he was, standing on the dimly lit landing; all mysterious and dark. My heart started to beat really fast and I was totally overcome with emotion and, to my shame, excitement. The children were asleep and the house was so quiet I could hear my heart pounding in my chest and could hardly breathe.

Against my better judgement I opened the door and as he moved forward and kissed me all common sense and doubt disappeared. He told me how much he missed me and that it wasn't him who had harmed the young shop assistant but his partner, who was a pure psychopath. So that was fine then, how could I have a problem with that Tam? My mind was numb and I suppose I got a bit carried away in the moment and I'm not sure exactly how we ended up in the bedroom but we did.

At first we sat on the edge of the bed and he was kissing me, laughing and telling me not to speak and I remember him putting his finger to my mouth and prising my teeth open and I could taste the bitterness from the tip of his finger on my tongue and I had the urge to vomit. His other hand was under my dress and I was becoming very uneasy but didn't know what to do because he kept repeating how much he loved me and wanted me. He pushed me onto my back and got on top of me and by that time I felt out of control. I tried to speak but the words caught in the back of my throat.

His voice was low and muffled and as he fumbled with my pants I tried to push him off and said we needed to stop but he put his hand over my mouth and I began to feel as if I was being suffocated. He carried on telling me how much he wanted me and that I had nothing to worry about. He was groaning and I couldn't control the panic that overtook me and became aware of the baby screaming in the next room. My skin was crawling and tingling and I thought that maybe that's what it should feel like. The trembling, the shaking with fear, or excitement, I didn't know what to do so I stopped resisting and then it was all over. Panicked and confused I looked at him for reassurance, he smiled and sat back on the edge of the bed adjusting his trousers and shirt. He was always very particular about the way he looked. I jumped up to go and see the baby who looked up at me and I felt overwhelmed with responsibility and shame. How could I have let this happen?

He told me he had to leave, to see Big Sammy, about a job and he would see me tomorrow. I looked at my watch and it was five minutes to nine. When he left I sat there, on the end of the bed, and could still hear one of the children crying in the next room so I pulled my dress down and then realised I still had my knickers on. I can't believe how stupid I was to think that maybe it was OK, maybe we hadn't actually done 'it', maybe I was making too much of what had been a bit of heavy petting. I wasn't sure what had happened but I did know that it would never happen again. Not with him anyway.

I got up and walked over to the window and could see down onto the main road and there he was, happy as Larry, looking as if he had won the biggest prize of all time in a bare knuckle fight. I waited a moment to see if he would turn and wave but he scuttled away, like the rat he was, without even a backward glance. The baby was still crying so I went into the other room, lifted her from the cot and held her close to me and as my tears fell silently onto her face she fell asleep again. Babies are so delicate and vulnerable aren't they?

When the couple got back about ten thirty and asked me if everything had been okay I said 'Yes, everything was fine'. The kids had been really good, no bother at all. I wondered if all kids were that well behaved and if it was always that easy. They gave me two pounds, thanked me and asked if I would do it again. I told them I wasn't sure and that I'd have to think about it because it had been a very new and grown-up experience for me but I would let them know.

The responsibility attached to that evening was too much for me and I never offered to babysit for anyone ever again. The next day when I saw him he kissed me and said I looked great and asked if I was okay. He told me to get myself all dolled up and he would take me out that night and I was to wear one of the suits he had left for me at my mum's house. When I got there and looked in my room there were six, beautiful designer suits, all the right size and in colours which suited me very nicely indeed. I wore a black velvet suit with a red vest top underneath. It was very modest and the trousers had a button, zip and would not be the easiest things to remove with one hand.

That evening I tried to talk about what had happened but he avoided it. I ate nothing and he told me to stop worrying and that no matter what happened he would stand by me. What did that mean? I felt very uncomfortable and resisted going back to his house by saying that my mum wasn't very well and I needed to go straight home. He replied saying he would go to one of the clubs in town to finish off the evening. At that point I couldn't have given a flying fuck where he was going or who he was going to see as long as he didn't come with me.

I saw him less and less in the following weeks and a girl I'd seen around the area came to my door and told me that I was ruining her life and begged me to stay away from him. She was very small with dark hair and large brown, haunted eyes. I felt sorry so sorry for her and asked her in for a cup of tea. As we sat there, on the end of my bed I wiped her tears and told her he meant nothing to me and I would have nothing more to do with him. When I thought about it, all I seemed to do in the time I was with him was cry, night and day, and wipe tears away. Then suddenly, there I was, sharing tea and pain with another lost lover weeping over spilled sperm.

The very next day I went to an agency, got a job with board and lodgings and moved off to live in another city. I decided at that exact moment I would take care of me, all by myself. Although my heart was breaking the day I left I felt lighter and knew it was the only thing to do in order to save myself. My heart had been destroyed and my tears dried up so there was no choice but to put on my size zero suits and move on to troubles new.

I came back when everything calmed down and heard that Robbing Hood had moved in with tiny tears and sometimes I thought it had all been a dream. I often feel when bad things happen it's easier to pretend it was a dream or a misunderstanding then I don't need to feel the shame or responsibility.

"How do you feel about staying here?"

What the fuck do you think I feel? It's a fucking hospital isn't it? Not my dream home by a long stretch. Although you've reminded me of my first, proper house. It was the first place we had stayed which had more than two rooms. It actually had an inside toilet, well a bathroom actually. Our name had come up on the council list because we were staying in the Salvation Army hostel on Clyde Street and my mum was delighted. We moved up the list fairly quickly because we were, of course, classed as homeless. See Tam, there's a lot to be said for being homeless.

The council house was like a dream come true with a front garden and a space at the back for drying the washing. It was going to be like 'Little House on the Prairie'. Although, the thought of leaving the hostel made me quite anxious and I was very upset the day we left because I actually enjoyed the routine. My Mum and I cleaned the dormitories which meant we got all our food for free. Imagine? Breakfast, lunch and dinner, every day, it was bloody marvellous. I wanted to stay there forever. Oh, and I nearly forgot supper, I had never had supper before in my life. A large cup of cocoa and a mint Yoyo - delightful! It did mean my dreams were very vivid though but that was fine. I started dreaming in colour after that. It was like going to the movies every night so it was a win win situation and I never wanted to leave.

They had also given me a room to study in after school and I had a single bed, all to myself, for the first time ever I didn't have to worry about waking up on someone else's wet patch. That reminds me of a story my brother told me not long ago about a time when we were young that he woke up and realised that he had wet the bed. My other brother was sound asleep on the other side and he rolled him onto it so that he would get the blame. Isn't that awful? Wee shite!

Anyway, let's get back to Utopia. The council informed my mother that the house would have to be occupied immediately. Someone had to move in as soon as she signed for the keys. Lying through her teeth she said to the council clerk that it would be absolutely fine as we could not wait to "inhabit our new residence." The guy was about seventeen and she insisted in calling him Sir and talking all posh. She used to do that with anyone who was behind a desk, had a stethoscope, or wore a tie. With the exception of my Dad that is because he always wore a tie. She usually referred to him as 'that dirty whoremaster'.

So anyway, in receipt of the keys, she went off to try and resolve the; no beds, no heating, no food, and no money issues by getting an appointment with the social security. Her next move was to contact my dad and ask him to stay at the house that night. Like a knight in shining, cashmere and wool mix, he arrived in a black hackney armed with a half bottle, six cans and a fish supper to take up his place as the defender of our four apartment, ground floor, garden flat.

Little did we know that the previous occupants had done a moonlight because of the impending release, from prison, of an arch enemy? This guy seemingly had a major grudge against our previous occupants and was out for revenge. My poor Da' was like a sitting duck when they arrived in the middle of the night with hammers and bayonets. They nearly beat him to death and he ended up in the Royal Infirmary.

I remember Captain Mary creeping into the dormitory during the night to telling my mother that the police were downstairs and needed to speak to her. When they told her what had happened she wanted to know all the details, especially if the door of the house had been locked when they took my dad away in the ambulance. My dad swore 'til his dying day that she had arranged the whole thing to get back at him for saying she had a fat arse. Like that was the only thing that bothered her about him.

When we eventually moved into the house it was November and freezing but one of the first things she did was put a seat out in the front garden for sunbathing. You've got to bless her optimism though Tam. The next morning it was gone - along with the garden fence. Can you believe it? Another night someone came in the window and stole all the money out of the gas meter. Lucky for us we didn't have much or they might have taken everything and we would have ended up with less than nothing. We also learned very quickly not to use the outdoor drying area because the only time we did put the washing out; it was stolen, washing line and all. Knickers – gone in a flash!

The summer holidays were great though and we spent most of the time outside and it seemed to be sunny and warm the whole time. We played on an old railway line down behind the house and made a swing from a discarded washing line we found. It was great fun and we spent hours swinging back and forth. It was such an adventure until one morning we went down and there were police everywhere. Someone had hung themselves from our rope during the night. I know this was really selfish but the only thing that bothered us was the fact we were not allowed to play there anymore and the chances of getting another washing line were slim. Unless we wanted to become thieves and murderers.

By New Year we had really settled in, gotten to know the neighbours, who turned out to be really friendly and were always at the door borrowing things. My mum used to go on these manic, cleaning fests. She would take these slimming pills that made her absolutely, unbearably energetic. She called them her black and white bombs. They were supposed to be appetite suppressants but made her explode with energy and enthusiasm. I remember this time she gave me one, just before a swimming competition at school and I won first, second and third place in nearly every race. I didn't sleep for about a week and never stopped talking. I was sick listening to me. Just like you most days Tam but at least you're getting paid and at least you get to go home at night. I was fucking stuck with myself all the time. Still am. It's bloody murder.

Honestly Tam, it was mental. People used to come to the door with things for sale and one time my mum got the chance to buy paint at a really good price from a guy who worked for the council. When we woke up in the morning she'd painted the top half of the hall orange and the bottom half bright green. It was like living on a corporation bus. She kept insisting how fresh it looked and saying how much she liked it but I'm sure she'd had an episode and couldn't even remember doing it.

There's this Scottish Tradition Tam and everything in the house has to be spotless for Hogmanay. It made absolutely no difference if the place was like a tip for the rest of the year but anything out of place at the stroke of midnight on New Year's Eve meant bad luck for the rest of the year and we didn't want that now did we? The last thing we needed was anything to interfere with all the good luck we'd been having.

My Mum said that it was bad luck not to have a pot of peas cooking at midnight on the 1st January. This was especially annoying because all the other families I knew had theirs with steak pie and potatoes and all we had with ours was vinegar. She used lots of vinegar and sometimes used to drink it straight out of the bottle as she said it was a fat buster and helped to repress her appetite. She even used it for cleaning the windows. Actually she was right about that and I use it to clean my mirrors and glass too. The peas though, she made that up because she'd probably spent all the money on drink.

Her home-made soup made was the best thing I ever tasted in my whole life. It was so thick that you could stand a ladle up in it. The very thought of it, never mind the smell used to make me feel hungry. One of her most prized possessions was an enamel ladle that she had bought for ten shillings down the Briggait, our local flea market, and it went everywhere with us and she had many uses for it. One time it even appeared in court. Oh, that ladle could tell a few tales.

Anyway, that Hogmanay my dad had shown up drunk as usual and they had the obligatory fight and she walloped him with her precious ladle. When the police arrived she said it was him that whacked her and he got arrested. As they were taking him down the stairs he was shouting, "Get me my lawyer, get me Beltrami." My Mum was funny and started shouting:
"Get him fucking Perry Mason, as long as you get him out of here!"

They took the ladle as evidence and she had to do without it for what seemed like a lifetime. It was dead funny because every time she made soup she spoke lovingly about the ladle and never once mentioned my Dad who had been banged up for six months. It was a great day the day she got it back we had a celebration and she made soup for a week. She also said that life had not been the same while it had been in custody. I'm sure it was the ladle she was talking about...she really loved that ladle.

"Have you experienced any decrease in your weight?"

No recently Tam but when I was nineteen I went to live in Italy and I put on about three stone, which was quite a lot as I am only five foot three. The day I left to go there should have been one of the happiest of my life but it was ruined because my mother was in hospital. She'd been in a coma for nearly three days and initially the doctors told us not to hold out much hope, but she pulled through. When she came round I was sitting by the bed holding her hand. She turned to me with a look of shame in her eyes and as they filled with tears as she told me how sorry she was to have messed up again.

Asking what time my flight was she said she hoped I hadn't missed it because of her. I explained how I wanted to postpone my trip until she was better and there was no question of me leaving her while she wasn't able to look after herself. After all, it had been there 'since the Romans' and there was plenty of time for me to travel. She got really upset and wouldn't hear of it and warned me that if I didn't get on the plane she was going to sign herself out of the hospital and refuse to take any further treatment. Some of her 'pals' were there and said it was for the best and they would look after her. These were women from the homeless unit and desperate to take over the house. There was no drinking or drunkenness tolerated in the hostel and they were looking for a sheebeen! You've probably never heard of a shebeen Tam. It`s place most like a pub where you barter goods such as drugs, fags and booze. Maybe that's where the word bar comes from, barter...bar?

What was I saying? Oh yes, my mum, the hospital. My mind was in turmoil and I knew that if I stayed she would keep her, insane, promise and leave the hospital. If she didn't accept treatment and counselling she would go right back to what she was doing before; about twenty-four cans a day Tam. Her new 'friends' also pointed out that the room I slept in had been promised to them and if I didn't go then they would have nowhere to stay and would be forced to go back to the hostel. I seemed to have no option and it was as if my mind had been made up for me. They were already running the show.

As I walked out of the hospital that day, with tears streaming down my face, I knew that, for the time being, leaving was the best option for everyone. I also thought that, maybe, if I stopped trying to fix her she would take responsibility and get better all by herself; get back to being her funny, brave, fabulous self. Walking out onto the street my feelings were mixed as my excitement about going battled with anxiety, leaving me with no sense of reality. I appeared to be going through the motions but had no control over what I was doing. I can barely remember the journey to Italy.

When I was there my brother would write me funny, four page letters and tell me stories about what he was up to and he made it all seem like such fun. He told me how he stayed out all night and didn't go to school, which he thought was great. He assured me that my mother's friends were very good to him and were always giving him money and making sure he always had fags. Cigarettes Tam, don't look too shocked, not actual homosexuals. They gave him tobacco. You're so shockable Tam, I love winding you up. Is shockable a proper word? I'm not sure. Imagine doing something all the time and not knowing how to spell it. They even gave him alcohol and he told me that he liked Super Lager the best. What? I thought, how many different types had he tried before coming to that decision? He was only twelve for god's sake.

He said that the party they threw for my mum when she got out of hospital was the best ever. It had lasted for four days and they had bought some great sausage rolls and pies. There were buskers who had come in off the street and the police came to the door at least five times. Each time they came some of the guys jumped out of the window and ran through the back gardens to escape. He thought it was brilliant and said that he couldn't wait to leave school and live the good life. Every day was Giro day, woohoo! Soon he was writing to me from a borstal.

Before we knew it though, the party was over, for all of us. La Dolce Vita in Italy had come to an end for me and time had been called at my mother's house. I can remember the very minute I got the call from my sister and my first thought was that my mother had died. So when she told me what had happened it came as a sort of relief. Actually, I can even remember what I was eating, pasta fagioli - all we seemed to do in that country was eat. To tell you the truth I was glad to be going home because I had started to make myself sick after each meal and I knew that was not acceptable behaviour. I didn't hesitate and got on the next flight to Glasgow.

It was a mess, Tam. One of the women who stayed in the house had died after overdosing on pills and drink. Although she lived there, in the house, no one had noticed for about three days. To tell you the truth, they probably only noticed because it was her turn to buy the drink. Some of them were still there when I arrived and I asked them all to leave. My mum looked at me, again with tears in her eyes and told me that she could not believe how fat I looked and asked me 'What the hell have you been eating while you were away? Can you believe that was the first thing she said to me?

Before I knew it we were back to normal and my time away became a distant memory. I got two jobs in order to pay back some of the debt and the weight just dropped off me and there was no need to concern myself with diets or any of that nonsense. You could say that I went very quickly from Humpty Dumpty to being one of the King's men as I put it all back together again!

Have you experienced any increase in weight?

Have you listened to a fucking word I've said in the past ten minutes?

Do you ever veer from the script?

Would you get the sack if you didn't ask me every stupid, banal, question on the bloody sheet?

I'm so pissed off with people who think they are qualified to give me advice and pretend to understand how I am feeling.

What the fuck does your job entail anyway?

Collating figures?

Is it mathematical?

She got four wrong so she is fine. More than ten wrong, she needs to come back.

All of them wrong?

What then, eh Tam, what do you do then? Does it all come down to numbers?

A Section bloody 24?

Is that the easiest way to conclude a session?

Is it?

Yes, come on, let's just say I get them all wrong and I'm nuts.
Just like Her.

What stupid bastard decides on these questions anyway?

Or do you all sit about having a laugh, with cups of herbal tea, eating bananas, suggesting all the discernible options that should be on the form?

What about you Tam what is your view on the fat issue? When will you inform the team of your considered, professional opinion?

Do you think it's important to know if she was ever fat?

Yes, that's very important to mental health. Isn't it?

She's a fat bastard, so that must be the reason she tried to top herself?

How is it relevant to anything that might be going on in this crazy, mixed up head of mine?

Well, I suppose it might be if that was why I was here, but I did not try to kill myself because I am fat, or because I'm too fucking thin.

Do you understand?

Do you even fucking care?

What time is it?

I've had enough of this shite for today. It's nearly lunchtime anyway.

What do you think I should have Tam, a nice, carbohydrate, fat and salt free salad?

"Do you find it difficult to concentrate?"

That all depends on what you mean because sometimes I have to concentrate in order to get fifty-two things done at the one time and have to write it all down. I've even found myself writing lists about lists and linking them by association. For instance, when it says on one list that I am going to 'make soup' you can be sure that there is another note that reads 'buy vegetables' or if I am planning to 'have sex' then it's bound to be written somewhere else that I have to 'shave my legs' or 'tidy up the crotch area'. Oh my god I have just remembered something!

One day a friend of mine phoned me to ask for advice because she had accidentally cut her lip, you know, one of the lips on her lady bits. She was so upset and she asked me what she should do to ease the pain. I didn't have a clue but when I'd had an episiotomy, that's where they... oh you know, okay. So anyway, they advised me to sit in a bath of salted water so that's what I suggested she did. She phoned me back later and was even more hysterical. I think a whole packet of salt might have been too much and her husband had come in early and found her in the middle of the kitchen sitting in the bowl. Her anniversary was ruined and all she had been trying to do was to make her fat china presentable. So sex was the last thing on her list for a while after that. She didn't speak to me for ages because when she phoned me crying I couldn't stop laughing and she didn't understand why but she kept saying:

> "My *whole* day has been spoiled."
> "My *whole* anniversary is a disaster."
> "My *whole* life is a mess."

I wanted to point out to her that if she had not tried to make her hole tidy in the first place, then she might have had a better time and anyway, I'm absolutely sure that men are not the least bit concerned what it looks like as long as they can insert and ejaculate. Tam, I'm not saying, for one minute, you are not capable of love but for the one eyed monster grooming is not first and foremost is it? You are probably just grateful to get laid and it might be a case of lust being blind, not love.

Where were we? Oh yes, concentration has never been my strong point and I usually have to write everything down and sometimes the list is that long it becomes quite depressing because there seems to be no end to it and I get really ticked off. Just the other day I found a list from a few years ago and all these awful memories came flooding back. Suddenly events that were buried deep in my mind were as clear as they were on the day they happened. It was as if I was looking at memory cards which exposed the exact times and locations of events that I would rather have forgotten forever but there they were and I couldn't focus on anything else:

Phone mum.
Take the kids to school.
Check on my Mum and see if she wants to do anything.
(No reply at the door.)
Go to the supermarket. (Separate list for that.)
Book Eye Test.
Phone mum again.
New jazz shoes from the dance shop.
Phone again.
Electrical shop for Hoover bags.
Collect girls from school and take them to dance class.

Phone mum!

Home.

That list was a very difficult one to adhere to because of the communication problem with my mother. She had stopped speaking to me completely because we were not going to her house on New Year's Eve. We had gone there every year since I got married but I had decided to have a 40th birthday party for my husband and she had refused to come. She was very stubborn that way but I had already invited everyone and was not prepared to cancel, but the thought of leaving her on her own made me feel a bit selfish and she played on that.

That night when I had everything ready for the party I thought I would give it one more go, so I got into the car and went to her house again. It was freezing and the house was in total darkness but I could see the key in the lock so I knew she was inside. I called her name through the letter box and pleaded with her to let me know if she was okay. I went outside and tried to see in through the window but the curtains were drawn. Not knowing what else to do I went over to a wall across from the house and just sat there, staring, waiting for some sort of sign that she was alive so that I could go home to the party.

After sitting there for what seemed like hours I was beside myself thinking about the best thing to do. Should I get someone to help me to break the door down or should I just go home because people would be arriving at mine soon? Yes, that's what I would do, go home, serve dinner, drink, sing 'Happy Birthday', pretend everything was fine and then come back. Then it happened! The bedroom light came on and I knew everything would be all right and that she was thinking about me and wanted me to enjoy myself. She had given me the go ahead to" bring in the bells " without her for the first time in my life.

It was funny because later that evening I told one of my friends about the 'sign' that my mother had so thoughtfully given me and she burst out laughing. She told me that I was bloody stupid and naive and that my dear mother could not give a fuck about anyone but herself. It had nothing to do with giving me permission to enjoy myself and not feel bad about her being alone but everything to do with her maybe getting up on time to make it to the pub. Some people can be very cynical can't they Tam?

I continued to try and 'gain entry' until the January 5th and when there were no further signs of life I asked one of her neighbours to help me to break in. The house was cold and very still and as I walked up the stairs I could feel my heart beating so hard in my chest that I thought I would suffocate. When I got to the bedroom door, I was overcome by the smell of urine and stale drink but I didn't want anyone else to go near her. Time seemed to stand still and I was shaking so much that I could hardly stand as I approached the bed and gently pulled back the cover. As I gently touched her cold, grey face she suddenly jumped up and shouted, "How the fuck did you get in here? Get the fuck out of my house."

She kept screaming and her eye balls looked as if they were about to pop out of her head and she did not seem to recognise me or Eddie but I was so relieved she was okay that I burst into tears. I stumbled down to the living room and sat amongst the mess and there were empty bottles and cans everywhere. It looked as if she had not eaten anything or taken any of her medication for days. My mouth was dry and my head was buzzing but I was so glad she was alive that I walked out and closed the door behind me. I could start to clean up the mess tomorrow. I would add it onto my list.

The next day before collecting the girls from school I stopped by the doctors and asked to speak to one of them about the situation with my mother. I sat there for an hour and fifty-two minutes before someone came to speak to me. By the time he came out to see me I was hysterical and pleaded with him to try to persuade her to get help. He said that she had been in the week before to see him and collect a prescription and she seemed absolutely fine so there was really nothing he could do. I got back into my car and looked at my list to see what I had to do next.

She died a month later.

Do you take time to relax?

I find it hard to relax. My husband relaxes by watching television, films, football, well anything really. Sometimes I think it's just to avoid dealing with me. Just the other night, or last week, maybe it was the week before, I don't remember. Does it matter when it happened? Sometimes I don't remember the order of things. They pop up in my mind and it's never clear when things occurred. I've thought of trying to write them down in chronological order but my brain just wanders and then... well, nothing really, blank!

Now there's a thought, maybe I should write all this stuff down. That might be relaxing. If I could just focus and put it down on paper, it might help my thought process. What if I wrote a book, what do you think about that Tam? I know you are paid to listen to all of this shite, but do you think anyone would actually pay for the privilege? I mean some days you come in and you are quite relaxed but you never seem quite so chilled by the time I leave, so maybe that would *not* be such a good idea. I don't want to upset people or make them feel uptight.

I remember one night trying to watch a film, it was supposed help me unwind and take my mind off things and I really did try to sit through it but it took me all my time not to scream, curl up and crawl onto the floor with exasperation. I was so agitated that my nails were bleeding at the base because I had bitten them so much. I remember getting up and wandering into the kitchen. My head was sore, I started to shake and feel really anxious. I felt so much pressure that my chest was tight and I clung onto the worktop; my knees felt as if they were about to buckle and my head was so muddled I felt dizzy and I fell to the floor. I sat there sobbing silently, feeling nothing but hopelessness and emptiness - but I had to go back in and watch the fucking film.

I took some Paracetamol and drank some wine that was left over from dinner. It was red and very strong and made me feel a bit sick at first but then, as I felt it travelling through my inside, all warm and soothing; I began to feel calm and went back to the sofa. Everything seemed to slow down and although the film wasn't making any sense I could stare at it without feeling the need to enjoy it or even understand the plot.

I didn't give a fuck or even care who the characters were, in the film, or in the room. It was the same way I felt about life really: nothing, no joy or hope, excitement or understanding - just despair, darkness, fear and an overwhelming sense of panic. About what? You may ask Tam, well, I still don't know and maybe I never will and anyway, is that not *your* job, to find that out?

Do you know what though? The sofas we have are really comfortable. They are massive and there would need to be something seriously wrong with someone if they couldn't settle down on those. The cushions are filled with feathers and when I got them at first they nearly drove me mad. What they do not tell you, at the point of sale, is that they must be plumped up every day. Every bloody day, I mean, who has time for that. I sent them a letter of complaint. It went something like this:

Dear "Definitely Fucking Sorry",

I Spoke to Janice today regarding the sofas that I bought from you that are driving me mad. I've hardly been in the house since I got them as they are scaring me half to death. Every time I look they seemed to have reallocated and become distorted. Now I am petrified to go into the front room for fear of what they might have turned into.

Janice explained to me in great detail that what I had bought was 'Soft Fit Furniture'. She very kindly and clearly explained the following to me: 'This type of furniture has to be plumped up at least twice a day.'

So, I asked Janice when the people would be around to do this?

No response from Janice.

Janice explained to me that she also had SFF (Soft F... Furniture) and plumped it up before she went to work and again when she came in.

I'd like to meet Janice because the cushions on my sofa weigh about six kilos each.

No need to spend time at the gym then, Janice. Where would you find the time anyway with all that 'fluffing up' going on?

I'd like to explain that I have a dog, two daughters and a husband that do not require any way near that level of attention. If anyone had explained to me that the furniture I was buying needed so much love, care and understanding then, would I have bought it? Would I F...!

I worked in retail management for many years and now that I am in another profession I sometimes miss the 'buzz' and thrill, of 'the big one'. Getting that sale that makes your day is one of the best feelings and can change the bulk of your pay packet. However, I did always know my product and would never have left a customer to discover anything inconvenient or unmanageable after the deal was done.

Product knowledge is very important but useless if it sits stagnant in one's head and is only recited and regurgitated after the fact.

Look forward to seeing someone from your Service Department soon.

Yours sincerely,

Exhausted Cushion Fluffer

So really, I try lots of things to help me relax but they all seem to turn into stressful situations that are out of my control.

Maybe I should try running. They say it releases those endorphin things in the brain. That's what I need, endorphins. The running thing could be a bit of a problem though because when I start to run I always think I'm about to wet myself with the excitement. Should I ever take it up seriously and decide to run a marathon then it would need to have Tena Lady Stops instead of water ones.

"Do you have problems making decisions?"

Well Tam, I remember that Christmas Eve when I had to make so many decisions I thought my head was going to burst wide open. Imagine the headlines: 'Christmas Eve Explosion - Burst Ginger Nut!' My daughter and I had spent most of the night at the hospital after my mum had accidentally taken too many painkillers. It was going to be a very busy day so I went home, got changed and then went straight to work. The day went by in a fog of embarrassed men grappling for anything that they thought would cost enough to keep a woman happy. A woman made me really angry by asking what I thought she should buy for her mother. What the fuck did I know about her mother?

When I finished work I headed over to the hospital and knew that the news would not be great because the silly woman had miscalculated and taken eighty, instead of eight, Cocodamol in the one day. A doctor stopped me before I got to the ward and asked me to go with him into one of the side rooms. He looked very young and seemed rather nervous. I asked him if he was okay and he smiled and introduced me to the other lady who had sat down beside him. She was some sort of counsellor but I don't remember as I didn't pay much attention to what she said. Most of these types talk a load of bollocks anyway. I was only interested in the facts regarding my mother. Was she okay and when would she be home?

Then he said it. He told me that my Mother was 'not going to make it'. What a bloody stupid thing to say. Make what? Stovies, steak pie, the bed? He informed me that because I was his point of contact it was up to me to inform everyone that, if they wanted to see her, they should get there soon as possible. What did he mean by everyone? Was I supposed to go out into the street and just shout it out to passers-by?

Being a next of kin is such an important job, isn't it Tam? No-one sits you down and tells you that they have a proposal for you and would you mind taking full responsibility for making everyone else miserable, on Christmas Eve, on the event of their death. In my experience it's usually an afterthought when someone says 'Oh by the way, I've put you down as my next of kin.' They stick a name on a form without thinking of the consequences to the nominee.

That's what I was now; my role had changed, and it was my job to inform everyone of the news, spread the word. I was no longer a mother, sister, pal, wife or daughter of a very funny and wonderful woman who was about to die; I was a point of contact.

>*"Hi, it's me (Point of Contact) how are you?"*
>
>*"Yes we are all good."*
>
>*"I'm just phoning to let you know…!"*
>
>*"By the way, Merry Christmas."*
>
>*"Give everyone a big kiss from me."*

I told him that he had to be joking. He must have seen my mother's case file? Every year, every holiday, every special occasion, every separation, every party seemed to begin with a drink and end up here, in this building. Six times that year she had been in that very same ward. He just looked at me and gave me a half smile while telling me again that the next twenty-four hours were crucial.

Feeling confused and angry but sorry for the young doctor, I left the hospital thinking what a terrible job he had. Imagine having to tell someone such bad news on Christmas Eve. When I got out onto the street I suddenly remembered my friend was bringing my younger child to meet me for the visiting hour. She adored her gran and had spent hours making a Christmas card that she was bringing with her and was so excited.

I had to decide what to say as there was no way I could tell her, there, in the middle of the street, why we weren't going in to the hospital. How could I explain this to anyone let alone my lovely, innocent, happy girl? The next thing I knew I was on the ground with my friend standing over me, stroking my face and telling me how sorry she was. I had collapsed in the car park and she had spotted me from her car.

I explained to my daughter that the visiting hours had been changed and she reminded me that I had promised to take her for a pizza. On the way home we stopped at Pizza Hut and it was very busy so I let her decide what we were going to eat. There is far too much choice in these places isn't there, Tam? I mean who needs a hundred different bases and thousands of toppings, besides the fact that you would need to be a mathematician to work out how much it is going to cost.

Something funny happened while we were waiting for the food. A little girl, who was sitting beside us, smiled at me and I stuck my tongue out at her and then she did the same back. Her Mother saw what she'd done and hit her on the head. I felt really guilty but decided not to explain and anyway my daughter thought the whole episode was hilarious. I was too numb to see the funny side because my mind was scrambled as I was trying to make sense of what was happening.

Soon the pizza was ready and the guy asked if we wanted any drinks with it and I told him that anyone would do, he could decide. By that point I was anxious to get home and consider who I should phone first. Was it best to make a list and go through it in some sort of order and tick the names off as I went along? Was alphabetical the best way to do it or should it be done by age or order of importance? What are the rules regarding these things? It would be great to have a book of etiquette that explains what to do in these situations especially if it had a chapter explaining how to do it without upsetting anyone.

On Christmas day I stayed in the house and let everyone else go and visit. It would have been selfish for me to be there, like the person who sits at the top of the table and looks as if they are in charge. I would let them all have their moment because I knew that I'd had more than my fair share of precious time and tomorrow it would be just me and her. They would all go home and wait for the next call which would give them further instructions.

One of the nurses that I'd got to know very well assured me that they would 'keep her going' 'til I got back on Boxing Day and I was not to worry. It's amazing that isn't it? Someone could be dead, to all intents and purposes and they can save them for a while, not forever, just 'til the family get there, to say their goodbyes. Secretly, every Christmas day I wish I could go back in time because I seriously thought they would keep her going forever. Had I known that they couldn't I would never have stayed at home making dinner and listening to her favourite music.

When I did go back to the hospital on Boxing Day I bumped into the young doctor and said to him that he must have thought that I was a right bitch speaking about my mother in such a rude manner but I explained that I had been really upset. He told me that he understood my distress and that when he had left the hospital that evening he had noticed me, clinging to a fence, bent over and sobbing in the street as he made his way home.

You see Tam, telling me the news about my mother had been the last task on the young doctor's list but to him it wasn't simply another tick of a box, job done. He seemed to really care, at least until his working day was over and he left the building.

"How do you view yourself?"

I've always thought of myself as being a good manager, an organiser, the type of person others would look to for advice and come to if they had a problem that needed fixing. I've always prided myself in being in control and always making the best of even the worst situations. Well, at least that's how I used to be, working full-time with two children and seeing to my Mum. That seems a really strange thing to say doesn't it 'seeing to'? The things you do for someone you love should be unconditional, done willingly and I have made it sound like something vulgar or a punishment. What a strange thing to say about what I did for someone I loved so much.

You see Tam everything became a struggle and it was very difficult to manage my life. When my Mum was well we would all be walking on eggshells and trying not to talk about the issues we were all dealing with. Drink, drugs and suicide were taboo subjects and best left alone. Although these were the diseases we were all suffering from in one way or another they were not up for discussion, full stop!

When things were good, she was a Godsend to me. Looking after the girls, cooking great food, and making us laugh. She was the funniest woman ever and I wish I could have recorded her best bits so that I could watch them over and over again, you know like they do on those reality shows? Everyone loved that part of her and she could redeem herself from even her most harmful assault when she made us laugh. She was immensely self-deprecating and very adept at making the most of her shortcomings.

For instance, all her teeth had fallen out when she was quite young and she hated wearing the false ones because they were far too big for her and she wouldn't go back to the dentist to get new ones. She only put them in for special occasions. My dad used to say that she looked like Shergar when she wore them, which was not helpful in getting her to comply. The trouble was that any time she spoke or laughed they would fall out so she usually ended up putting them into her coat pocket. She used to joke about not knowing where to put a sweet or a crisp, in her mouth or in her coat pocket. To tell you the truth she actually looked much better without them.

She used to terrify my young brothers by turning her back on them and putting the teeth into her mouth and then turning back round and smiling at them. The poor wee souls used to be terrified and hide under the bed. Her and her stupid friends used to think this was hilarious. When I think about it now, it really was quite cruel.

She was always telling people how proud she was of me and how she was amazed by the way in which I looked after my children. She would brag about my 'high powered' job and all the lovely things I had, my perfect house, my nice car and my lovely life. However, after a few swallows, that all changed. She would look me up and down and say how uncomfortable she felt in my 'too tidy home' and that my gorgeous husband was not all he was made out to be.

He thought she was a wonderful woman and used to go to her house on his day off to keep her company. He also raved about the food that she dished up for him. He would stay for the whole day even though she didn't even have Sky telly. That's how much he loved her.

She would tell me how he been at her house all day and all he did was sit and stare at the telly. Then she'd say that she believed that he thought he was too good to talk to her and that he was only ever concerned about himself. This was the same man who missed out on going to golf tournaments and football matches because he insisted being with her at times when she was deemed to be too lonely and vulnerable to be left on her own. He thought she was wonderful and would have done anything for her.

I remember getting my first answering machine for the phone. I got it in order to monitor my calls because I was fed-up being tortured by drunken parents telling me how much they loved each other. They would drone on to me for hours on end and yet they would not speak to each other. At first I loved it and would get in from work and be so excited to hear who had called and then it became a tool of dread and all the joy of my new technology was flushed away, with one very short comment.

I remember getting in from work one evening and pressing the button while taking my daughter out of her pram and hearing a message that was both hurtful and unjust in its ignorance:

> *'It's that bloody machine again. I fucking hate it. Who the hell does she think she is? Sitting in her big house like the queen of bloody Sheba.........?'*

I felt sick as she let loose her venom. She must have phoned to speak to me and left her phone off the hook. She continued with her rant but I could not bear to listen in case she said anything horrible. I'm sure she was just kidding anyway. She was such a joker. I never spoke to her about it because I know she would have been really embarrassed. It's funny isn't it Tam, a piece of equipment I got to relieve myself of a stressful situation ended up making things worse.

Whenever I was out with my mum and someone gave me a compliment or said I looked nice, or smart, she would smile but say under her breath 'She always bloody does.' It was just her way. It got to the point that when I bought anything new it would go straight into the wardrobe as it made me feel uncomfortable showing her the nice things I could afford. I felt guilty, as if I was doing something wrong by deliberately shoving my happiness in her face.

I suppose the view that we have of ourselves is never quite the same as the one that other people have of us. I used to consider myself to be very confident and self-aware but now I'm not so sure of who I am or who I thought myself to be in the past. Maybe I was pretentious and put up a front in order to make everything look okay in the hope it would all blow over and that some sort of human tragedy might be diverted for the time being. It must have been a big act really, a coping mechanism. How would you interpret my feelings about myself Tam? After all you're the expert. Can you help me recall some of the 'best bits' because my mind only seems to be equipped to tune in to the heartbreak channel?

Tam's Return From Holiday

Hi Tam, it's so good to see you back. The other psyche professional I saw when you were away was very odd. His name was Miguel and his accent was so strong I could hardly make out a word he was saying. He was worse than you. It seems to be par for the course here. I seem to be the only person with a local accent and that seemed to be up for debate with him as he seemed to think that I had come from somewhere else.

He had a really kind face though, the kind of face that looks concerned but puzzled at the same time. There was a certain serene, tolerant and uncomplaining aspect of his countenance that was quite reassuring. Later though he became all upset and seemed a bit befuddled. I don't think he was very well.

First of all, he asked me what I liked about living here. I explained that I saw it more of a pit-stop than an actual abode and that I hoped to be going home as soon as possible. I said to him that being here was less of a choice and more of a necessity. He said he totally understood but wondered why I wanted to go back as I might be in danger. Danger of what I thought, wearing out the new sofas?

Then he asked me if I had made any friends since my stay here. I explained that most of the time I only speak to the receptionist and then I'm here, for a couple of hours, with you. It's not that I have a problem with the inmates or anything like that, I'm sure that they are all very nice, in their own special way. Miguel seemed disappointed that I had not integrated more.

He then started probing about what I remembered about my life before. I was very confused by this and asked him if he meant before today or before the episode? He seemed quite excited by that and said we would focus on what happened to lead me here. Finally, we seemed to be getting somewhere. Then he asked me the next question and I thought to myself, where does he think he is?

"What was it like living in a war zone?"

That's what he said, seriously, I know that living in the East End is not ideal but I would hardly call it a war zone. Although, the period leading up to the cup final is pretty dire and then there's the Orange Walk. That can be pretty noisy. Or did he mean before that, when I lived in The Gorbals? If you have ever read 'No Mean City' then you would probably think of it as a bit like Armageddon but that has all changed now with the regeneration and everything.

There are lots of new houses and many of them are occupied by people who come in to work in the City. They buy them as second homes, which is probably cheaper than renting a parking space for a whole year. They are mainly professional people, lawyers and the like. There are lots of criminal lawyers in Glasgow, you know. There is an unlawful element but it's the same with most big cities, it's all relevant.

"It's good to see that you are engaging with the history and the culture of the city but I'm interested to know what happened to you in Afghanistan?"

"What are you talking about?" I asked him. I know that sometimes I tell fibs and embellish my stories but I only do that when I think you are getting a bit bored Tam. I've never once said that I lived in Afghanistan or Uzbekistan or any other 'istan', as that would be taking things too far. I know nothing about those countries. I've never even been in the Red Road flats.

Anyway, it all became clear soon enough. The poor guy was a bit stressed and had gone into the wrong building and had mistaken me for an asylum seeker. He wasn't far wrong was he Tam? He was off work for two weeks after that. Wonder what happened. Seemingly, I was the last thing on his list of things to do that day. No-one has seen him since. Maybe he went back to Spain? Maybe Glasgow just wasn't for him.

"What do you fear?"

There are not many things that frighten me but sometimes I am overwhelmed by a fear of nothing in particular. It's hard to describe and even more difficult to understand that there can be a dark force inside that you can't touch or channel into. Especially because mine lives in there with my imagination and I'm in control of that to a certain extent. It's as if there are two defence mechanisms fighting for control of my ability to function: one that thrives on fairy stories and the other based on a Hitchcock thriller. Take my fear of public toilets for instance, that is an internal fear that can become a very public reality.

The tenement blocks where we lived usually had outside toilets and there was one on each landing which was shared by three families. So, three to four people in each family meant that it was used by at least twelve people at the one time. I don't mean that they all went in together but I tell you this, I never, ever went on my own if I could help it. There was a lot of shit for one bog to contend with by anyone's estimation and sometimes they would get really blocked and all the waste would spill down the stairs. It was disgusting. I hated it and I still become very anxious if I have to 'go' in a public place.

They say that some fears can be hereditary but no one else in my family seemed affected by this toilet terror that I had. My dad certainly wasn't because he used to let the whole building know when he was going for a 'visit to the box office' as he called it. He would knock on the doors and tell them that he would be there for a while and if any of them 'needed' then he would let them go first. When he was sober he was very polite and had a dreadful fear of offending anyone. There was a great sense of camaraderie about sharing in the community at that time.

If ever I did have to go on my own I found it especially nerve-wracking to the point where I would nearly shit myself, so I would hum or sing really loud to let people know I was inside. They could probably hear me from the other end of the street when I think about it, and the more nervous I felt the louder it got. I still do it you know, whenever I'm in a public convenience. I remember one night in particular when I woke up with rumbling pains in my tummy and everyone in the house was fast asleep. After spending about ten very anxious and sweaty minutes of trying to wake my sister to go with me I realised that in order to preserve my dignity I had to face my fear alone.

Sometimes in a real emergency there was an excuse for using a bucket in the house but I would have exploded before I would have gone down that road. At a push I could have maybe done a number one but never, ever, a number two. The toilet was kept locked and each family had their own key which was about the size of my forearm and it lived on a nail by the front door and the toilet paper, if we had any, was on the tallboy. Not an actual boy you understand, Tam - it was a chest of drawers that was usually found in the bedroom of a house but we didn't have any of them so ours was in the hall.

That would be funny wouldn't it if there was a big, lanky boy there, waiting in the hall, whose sole purpose it was to hold a roll of toilet paper. I bet there are some stinking rich people who pay for services like that. I've heard that Prince Charles' valet actually wipes his bum for him. Wonder if he's tall and is kept in the bedroom, or the hall -

or maybe it's a girl. You never know with these royals, do you Tam?

I bet they also have toilet paper made from cashmere wool from goats and from organic silk worms, whereas all we got was thread-worm from using old newspapers. I often craved the relief that the cheap, scratchy paper gave me when the itch became too much to bear. San Izal was like the patron saint of poor, larva ridden butts. That would have been a great marketing slogan wouldn't it Tam? Sorry, where was I? Oh yes, me, sore tummy, during the night.

Having collected the tissue and key I opened the front door and secured the Yale lock so that I would not get shut out, because that would have been a disaster. It was freezing and I thought about going back to get a jacket but decided that I would be quick and didn't bother. There were thirteen steps and because I was superstitious I always hurled myself off the third one from the bottom because I thought that some disaster would befall me if my foot touched the last step. Better to be safe than sorry. Although, I did tumble a couple of times, spraining my ankle and wrist which wasn't very lucky.

So, having conquered the stairs in the dark, there I was, negotiating the door, which was made of heavy, solid wood, when I dropped the toilet paper. It rolled down onto the next landing just as the door swung open and knocked the key out of my hand. By that point I was touching cloth and had no choice but to opt for the media option which had been carefully cut into squares and hung on a piece of string for the use of everyone. I still don't know who did that because I don't ever remember anyone in our house sitting down, like something from an episode of Blue Peter, preparing the weekly edition for communal consumption.

The only way to shut the door from the inside was with the key so I had to leave it open. So there I was, sitting on the throne, totally crapping myself in full view of whoever might be passing by at three in the morning. I was really lucky that no one did and it was such a relief that my internal discomfort was now an external reality. Then to my horror I saw that the water in the bowl had frozen over and there it was, my steaming faeces, sitting there, staring back at me.

I knelt down and prayed, right there and then, that God would help it stay warm enough to melt the ice and help it on its way. When it was inside, although it caused me physical pain I wasn't frightened by it, but now that it was out there I was, literally, scared shit-less. I also knew that if I flushed there was the possibility that it would overflow and then the stairs would be a right slippery mess and I'd probably break my neck trying to get to school the next day because of my issue with the uneven number of stairs.

After waiting a while for some kind of sign from above I resigned myself to the fact that it was going nowhere fast and anyway who would even know it was mine; it's not as if it had my name on it or anything else that would link it to me. Even if someone wanted to make a big deal out of it there was no testing of DNA or anything like that in those days. All I had to do was rescue the key and the toilet roll, put them back in their rightful places, go back to bed and no one would be any the wiser. Or so I thought.

In the morning when I got up and was getting ready for school I heard one of the neighbours asking my mum how I was. She was worried about how long I'd spent in the toilet during the night and had waited until I was safely back in the house before she went back to her bed. My mum thanked her and asked her how she had known it was me and she explained that she had been woken up by my stupid singing.

"Do you ever have any thoughts of death or suicide?"

Well, hasn't everyone, it doesn't make you a bad person? Yet it is important to separate thoughts and actions. Taking your own life doesn't resolve anything or make you feel better because when you are dead then you don't feel anything at all. So it sort of defeats the purpose I think. People can make moral judgements about it but if the pain someone is suffering is far greater than their ability to cope then who is to say if it is wrong or right to take what ultimately belongs to them?

I remember after my mother died a doctor asking me that very same question and I was completely honest with him, which was probably not the best idea. I explained that sometimes, when I felt really low, I experienced flashing images of myself in various stages of resourcefulness. One tableau was of me, hanging from a rope suspended from the banister of the stairs in my house. Another was me lying unconscious in a blood red bath. Both of these images were really quite disappointing and totally lacking in imagination to tell you the truth. Actually, if I had made it up then the scenarios would have been much more interesting and metaphysical.

He was not my regular doctor, one of those locums who always try desperately to fit in. He looked at me with a very concerned expression and asked me if there was any actual episode where I had tried to kill myself. What a stupid fucking thing to say. If he knew me at all then he would know that I am very thorough and if I *had* tried to 'do myself in' then I would not be sitting there having the conversation. I tried to back track and told him that I was making it up and that I thought it was funny. He obviously had no sense of humour. Where was Doctor Regular, who couldn't care less, when I needed him?

So, after the longest consultation ever, he gave me my prescription which I took to the chemist in the Asda in Parkhead. This turned out to be another massive error for which I had to pay for the next four weeks. The girl behind the counter asked me a couple of questions, gave me a pen to sign with, without even looking at me. There was no proper waiting area and no seats. As I stood there looking around I was aware of others standing in the same area. We all shared a common thread; we were not just in Asda but in God's waiting room, to be judged by all on our flaws and weaknesses.

I could tell that a couple of the other consumers were waiting for their approved dose of Methadone. It upset me that they should be standing there in that exposed incarceration looking helpless, vulnerable and self-conscious in their daily ridicule. The fact that they are called over and taken into a cubicle does not take away from the scorn and contempt that can be sensed from the fellow shoppers. It's a bit like the old days when people were forced into stocks and had things thrown at them. Maximum humiliation being the order of the day! Instead of being immobilised by shame they should be proud that they are at least trying to help themselves.

On the other hand, there are some who have already had a fix and are simply there for a top up. Some of them might even be so desperate that they will hold it in their mouths 'til they get outside and regurgitate it into the mouth of a paying friend for a pound. These victims are trance-like and walk with knees bent and stare blankly with eyes that have deathlike expression, half covered by eyelids that lack any strength or willingness to stay open.

Suddenly the girl behind chemist counter shouted my name and said:

"Do you know that you have to get these weekly, dear?"

Mortified and confused I very quietly went over and asked her to explain what she meant. It turned out that Doctor Detail, with whom I had never consulted before in my life and who did not know me from Adam, thought that I was a high risk and not responsible enough to have twenty-eight pills in my possession at any one time. Where he got that idea I will never know! This meant that I had to go every week and suffer this indignation from a jumped up little Oompa Loompa who had no concept of what she put people through in her line of duty.

So there I was two aisles away from a shelf where I could pick up sixteen Paracetamol for 32p, which is the maximum amount that you are supposed to be allowed. Or is it thirty-two you can buy in one go? I'm not sure. I'm certain that they would have noticed immediately if I had gone to the check-out more than once because everyone is so bloody careful these days aren't they Tam?

> *"Oh, excuse me, did you not just buy some of these at checkout 5 six and a half minutes ago and did we not see you on CCTV buying some from Superdrug just around the corner. So, I must inform you that we are about to call the police and have you arrested."*

Every check out assistant in the country is now in line for a job as a procurator fiscal. What a bloody palaver. For the next month I had to go there, in disguise I may add, in case the growling girl was on guard, to get my 'script'. Did you see what I called it there? I've got a whole new lingo now that I am down with the junkies.

That month passed very quickly and I took the following one to a far more discreet pharmacy in another part of the town. Soon I was feeling much better and hardly noticed the weeks passing by. So much so that I kept forgetting to go and get the pills so I started to take half and that way they would last twice as long and save me some trouble. Isn't that clever, self-medicating? I think I could be a doctor. I mean it can't be that difficult. Just sitting there, listening, and ticking boxes. How hard can it be to earn that crust? I wouldn't want a big fat arse though. That must be a downside of the job, eh Tam?

When I think about it the doctors were taking such good care of me that they let me enjoy myself for another six months before anyone clicked. Well actually it was me who told the doctor. I decided to consult with him and ask if it was maybe time to cut down again. Guess what he said Tam? Go on guess? *He* asked *me* what I thought. Can you believe it?

Another thing I can't understand is what kind of training those despots on the reception desk must get? Are they sent to Guantanamo Bay to brush up on their skills? If one of them had taken my order over the phone in the first place, then I would not have had to suffer that entire month of trauma in the first place. I'm convinced that those tyrants all wanted to be doctors but didn't have the caring gene. So instead they became dictators with the absolute power of prescription and appointment.

They sit there, with their phones and computers of mass domination, unrestricted by compassion or common sense and make the patients' life a misery. It's a wonder anyone ever gets to see the skill of a qualified, general practitioner. What skills do you think are important to be a good doctor? You're a sort of doctor aren't you Tam, but you're a lot are more interested in statistics and filling in forms aren't you? Where exactly do you come in the hierarchy of doctor hood? I think personally that with all the cutbacks in the NHS that all the boundaries are being blurred. Nurses are doing the work of doctors and before you know it the doctors will be clever enough to work on the reception desk!

"Any fluctuations with your libido?"

Well Tam, libido is one of those things that sound quite exotic, like a cocktail, or something that you would ask for in a posh restaurant or in one of those very la-di-dah designer stores isn't it.

"Do you have any libidinous sweaters in stock?"

That's just reminded me of a guy I used to go out with who would break into a sweat at the thought of a kiss, never mind the prospect of a lustful interaction. Sex with him would have been impossible as we would have been slipping all over the place. The thought of him, naked, panting and dripping all over me gave me the dry physical, in all respects. Maybe it's his fault that I have trouble easily enabling this most basic human instinct and need someone very patient to tender my fossil and agitate it into frenzy.

Also, libido is supposed to be related to an urge to reproduce so how does that work with you guys? Now tell me the truth Tam, how many blokes do you know that, when they have a hard-on, become ecstatic about the fact that they are just about to make a baby? Exactly! Men are not really deep thinkers when it comes to sex. The thought of a uterus does not enter their minds when they see a vagina. Their primal senses take over and they become ethereal beings howling like banshees on a hairy mound.

Women on the other hand can become so desperate to have a baby that they go a bit mental and develop all the symptoms of pregnancy, and in extreme cases even have a hysterical labour. I had a friend who had not had a boyfriend for four years and she was convinced she was expecting. I humoured her until the point where she asked me to be her birth partner. WTF was my initial reaction but seemingly if the patient is convinced that there is no baby then the symptoms stop. I couldn't believe that the doctor was going along with this nonsense and had booked her in for an ultrasound so that she could see her empty womb.

The day we went for the scan was the last day I saw her. She didn't die or anything like that she just never spoke to me again. You see those foetal portraits are vague at the best of times but this was just ridiculous. There we were her looking at the monitor, me eye-balling the doctor and thinking, 'are you fucking kidding me?' And there *he* was looking at me as if to say 'you're her friend, *you* tell her that her vessel is empty'.

Well, it was all too much for me and off I went. I laughed so much that they had to give me oxygen before eventually escorting me off the premises. It was hilarious. Don't get me wrong I did have some sympathy for her but if she'd taken my advice in the first place and realised that the problem was, in fact, her deep rooted and unfulfilled sexual desire, then we would still be friends.

Libido was never mentioned in our house and I remember my mum trying to explain 'it' to me, whatever 'it' was, but she was usually very nervous or very drunk and it always came out so wrong. I can think of one instance when she was standing beside the kitchen sink and there she was, with her washing board, furiously rubbing away at the crotch of her knickers. She had nearly worn it away by the time she was finished trying to illuminate me about 'dirty stuff'. I thought she was talking about her dirty smalls and wondered why she was so red in the face.

She would start to talk about the birds and the bees - *actual* birds and bees. She tried to explain how the bee was always in charge and pounced on the flower and sucked the life out of it and then moved on to another flower. She said it was important to be careful or I would lose all my honey and would be no use if another decent bee wanted me. Well, that was about right; when I think about the B... that eventually did my deflowering I realise that love had nothing at all to do with it.

When I met my husband it was all so different and we were very close and intimate right from the start. The first time I had an orgasm I cried for about a week. The poor lad was very confused indeed. At such a happy time in my life though, all I could think about was how much I wanted to kill the repellent parasite that had infiltrated my trust, love and my heart that first time.

There are times though when the sight of women's private bits can literally shrink a man's libido forever. One night my man came in after working a twelve-hour shift and I was still up waiting for him, which he usually saw as a signal for sex - we have a code you see. Anyway, that was not the case and it turned out to be a very different, sort of organic encounter.

I had to explain to him in a very self-conscious manner that I had a tampon that got lodged while I had been swimming. I had not long had a baby and it must have had enough room to whirl around and I could not find the string to pull it out. I had been trying all evening to no avail. I really should have been doing more of those pelvic floor exercises, the midwife told me that I should do them every day but I was always so busy.

We got it out eventually and it was such a relief because you can die from that you know? Toxic Shock Syndrome it's called isn't it? I wonder if anyone has ever tried to kill themselves with a tampon. The thing is they are really very dangerous and I think you should be warned before you are allowed to use them. I think that if people, women mainly, although I'm reliably informed that men also have a use for them, knew the risks associated they would be very reluctant to try them.

On the packet it is suggested that they are stored away from heat and moisture so that bacteria can't grow on them. Then it clearly states that you are to shove it into your vagina which, most of the time, well before the age of fifty, is quite hot and wet. This sadly is no longer the case because my honey pot is now a cool, dark, lonely place which is vacant and about as useless as the box of tampons under the sink.

"Do you have any hobbies?"

A while ago I decided to go away for the weekend and incorporate two of the things I enjoy doing most, walking and going to the theatre. In fact, when I got home, I decided to write down some of the things that had happened. Well not actually how they happened but my recollection of events.

Someday I would like to be a writer, when I am more focused, when my head is not so busy. When I got back from that weekend I felt great, really calm and content. I have a copy in my bag would you like to read it?

Public Transport

Today I'm going to Arran which is a beautiful Island off the east coast of Scotland. My daughter is an actor and is in a play there. I've seen it three times in Glasgow but I view this as a chance to walk, eat, take in the stunning scenery and remove the city from my lungs, mind and hair.

Although, when I spend any more than thirty minutes beside the sea my hair resembles that of a ginger cat that has been accidentally left in the freezer all night. More about hair later. My first mode of transport (MOD) is the ferry from Ardrossan.

With anticipation I get on board and the first thing I do is find out where the toilet is. This has been a habit of mine since I wet myself on a dentist's chair when I was nine. Under the influence of the rubber gas mask I dreamt that I was searching for a toilet. My search took me along the long corridors and through all the dormitories in the Salvation Army Hostel on Clyde Street.

Eventually I found a very large Doc Martin boot beside a bed and proceeded to pee into it.

To my great embarrassment I woke up, back on the dentist's chair, to find my knickers and dress soaking wet. The dress was not even mine. It was borrowed from a neighbour and the pants were co-owned by my sister and me. My mum said it was groovy to share undergarments so we were dead chuffed and revelled in telling everyone how trendy and new age we were.

So, back on the boat, in the security of knowing where the toilet was I found a comfy spot near a window in full view of an emergency exit and of the coffee bar so that I would not waste good writing time waiting in the queue that was sure to form, and the exit was in full view. By the time we sailed off I was prepared for any eventuality; coffee, toilet, escape in an emergency and my new career as a writer.

A lovely, elderly couple came and asked if the two seats beside me were free and I assured them that they were and they were more than welcome to park themselves there for the duration of the trip. Half way into the journey I was aware of a chinking and sucking noise to my right and was horrified to turn and see the couple getting tore into each other.

There they were munching and sucking away at each other's faces and having a right old grapple. He had his hand down her twin set and she had her arthritically deformed hand on his stained crotch. It was disgusting! Suddenly there was a joggle and I realised that I had, in, fact nodded off. The couple smiled at me and asked if I was okay. Nearly there!

On arrival, I got off the ferry and enquired as to where my hotel was. A lovely wee man told me it was within walking distance and gave me directions. Aye right. Forty-five minutes later I was at the hotel having walked up the hill and around the bend and ending up nearly back at the main road. That was one thing to take off the list of things to do because I think he had sent me up Goat's Fell. So that's what entertains the locals here, telling us townies where to go?

Got changed and headed down to the Town Hall to give other daughter the antihistamines that were requested, only to be told that there was nothing on there that evening but there was something on in Lochranza. How do I get there then? Not falling for that one again I would just get a taxi. Twenty quid later, arrived at destination.

Pubic Hair

The next day I was feeling great and decided to go for a swim. This menopause is child's' play and I don't know what all these other women moan about. My top feels a bit big for me though and I'm not sure if my boobs have dropped or the halter strap has stretched by about four inches.

Get into the pool and nearly have a heart attack as the water feels about -2C but the good thing is that my bosom jumps back into place. Try to focus and breathe cautiously as my chest feels tight and my skin is turning blue. Once I start to defrost and swim all is well and the feeling starts to come back to my arms and legs. Fantastic! Soon I'm on my eighth length and get my second wind and know that I will probably manage twenty or so.

After twenty-one lengths and forty-five minutes I feel exhilarated and decide it's time to call a halt. I pull myself up the stairs and feel as if I weigh twenty stone and fall to my knees at the side of the pool. One of the attendants comes to my aid and I insist that I'm fine and just a bit off kilter. I then stagger and lurch towards the changing rooms and have to sit down for five minutes before going to the shower. Glad that I've not broken my nose this time.

I hate these communal showers and there are two pubescent pieces of some mother's litter sniggering and gibbering in front of me. I turn away from them and bend down to lift my shampoo and to my dismay see that my ginger pubes, that had been all nice and neatly tucked into my bikini bottoms, have escaped.

They are now poker straight and have grown by about three inches and are sticking out of the sides of my bikini bottom like the hanging gardens. This gives a whole new meaning to growing my fringe out quickly, which has been a dilemma of mine in the past. Looking on the positive side, how many mentalpausal women still have healthy and vibrant coloured pubes to boast of?

This reminds me of how functional and effective pubic hair can actually be. In addition to its indication of sexual maturity and the need for the reduction of chafing during sex, it has various other uses. For instance, I remember staying in a very basic B&B and there was only a slither of soap. I did not have a cloth with me and very industriously soaped up my pubic hair and invented my own natural, organic scrunchy.

I felt very proud of my improvised cleansing tool and wondered if this could be marketed for a profit. Not sure exactly what it is that I would be marketing though as it would be hard to copyright someone else's privates. I could however, find a way to develop, patent and market the idea. Need to think that one through a bit more!

Before my next visit to the pool there is a very definite need for modification of the crotch area. My investigation of the possibilities involves conversation with daughter number one. She suggests a Brazilian, which is her preferred choice but, the leg over the head part puts paid to that for me. I think I will opt for the 'Landing Strip' as the name suggests fun for hubby as well and that will make it a double whammy. Pardon the pun.

Restyling was also suggested in the form of a 'Faux-hawk' which is where the condemned tresses are simply fashioned instead of removed. That nevertheless would not resolve my fully grown lady garden predicament. Why does hair always seem to generate such crisis? Sea, sand, wind and fringes are all dilemmas faced on an on-going basis universally.

The other day I was talking to my daughter about my new haircut and suddenly she started to cry. It was my actual head hair this time and not the tresses previously mentioned. I asked her what was wrong and she began to explain that my hair discussions had always been a problem for her and that I was, in fact, a 'Hair Whore'.

I was stunned and could not identify with this label that she had given me. She went on to explain that since she could remember my post haircut chat had nearly driven her insane. To the point that she nearly wished that my stress levels would increase so much that I might get alopecia:

"I like it but...."

"See this wee bit here? Do you see what I mean?"

"It's a bit too short. What do you think?"

"I wanted it a bit shorter."

"It's a bit too tidy."

"I hate the way hairdressers dry my hair."

"That's the last time I go there."

"He talks incessantly."

"That girl is a bit funny. She never says anything."

She told me that once she even booked a week's holiday in Gran Canaria as she felt one of my haircuts coming on.

Too taken aback to say anything I touched her hair, which was a bit dry and in need of a mask, and told her that I had no idea and wouldn't bother her any more with my hair emergencies. Her phone rang and she got up and went to her room.

Thinking about what she had shared with me I decided that instead of my usual frantic hair episodes, which usually started with me waking up like Cherie Blair after an election result, I would be pro-active. From now on I would book in advance, take a photo and be more specific about my requirements.

Having decided on this tactic I went up to her room and asked her for the number of her hairdresser at which point she screamed and threw a pink fluffy cushion at me and told me to get out. Obviously the bad mood was the result of that call. I'm presuming it must be boy trouble!

THE END
(for now)

What do you think, Tam? I know it needs editing in bits and the first two chapters don't really gel but I can work on that. Up until now you're the only person that's seen it. I wrote all of that in about ten or fifteen minutes and then I lost my train of thought. That was last year and I keep meaning to try again but it's hard to find inspiration. Not much goes on in the one room, with just me in it. Anyway, I'm much better now and I'll be going home soon. So excited I can hardly sleep!

Do you have any significant or unusual dreams?

Last night I dreamt I was dying and it was beautiful!

Like summer and winter sparkled with spring.

I was swimming in snowflakes towards a bright, welcoming moon.

Postcard from the edge!

Hi Tam,

Sorry I couldn't make it today but I thought I'd write you this note so you can tie up all the loose ends and tick all the relevant boxes.

The pills you prescribed for me seemed to do the trick, when they eventually kicked in, but I know that we're simply delaying the inevitable.

When I got home everyone was walking on eggshells and trying to do what they thought was right to keep me on my pathway to recovery. I explained about my recurring dream where I am being swept away and have no strength or willingness to fight back.

So here I am on the holiday they booked as a surprise.

It's 5am Tam and everyone's asleep. I'm tiptoeing off before they wake. It's that time of day when the moon has just gone in and the sun is reaching out. The sand dunes are extraordinary and the water is crystal clear. The feeling of the cool, early morning sand under my bare feet is just what the doctor ordered!

Goodbye Tam, thanks for listening.

It's been a blast!

Mx

margaretmazzone@hotmail.co.uk

Printed in Great Britain
by Amazon